He walked to the steps and leaned against the wall. "You didn't answer my question. You always dress like that when you're sleeping alone?" he asked, his voice low and husky.

"Yes."

Alexander pushed off the wall and climbed the stairs, stopping one step away from China. He ran the back of his hand across the front of her stomach. "Nice. Does it come in other colors?" China shivered and took a step back. A slow, sexy smile crawled across Alexander's face before he took a step forward. "What other colors do you have, China?"

"Wh-white," she whispered. China cleared her throat. "What do you want, Alex?"

Alexander removed the glass from China's hand and finished off the contents. He sat it on the step, then pulled the towel from China's head, allowing her damp hair to hang free. He dropped the towel, cupped China's face with both hands and kissed her passionately on the lips. Alexander let them breathe and said, "You know what I want."

Dear Reader,

I'm excited to introduce everyone to my new series, The Kingsleys of Texas. The Kingsley family is fiercely loyal to each other, and their business. They have rich and powerful friends who come to their aid when called, friends that you just might know. The Kingsley brothers are gorgeous, very sexy and extremely wealthy.

In *Always My Baby*, best friends Alexander and China work together to defend their company against bogus charges brought by the EPA. In the process, these friends cross into the uncharted territory of passion. It's exciting to see the sexy measures one takes to ensure the survival of their transformed friendship.

I love interacting with my readers, so please let me know how you liked Alexander and China's story. You can contact me on Facebook or Twitter. Coming soon, the youngest Kingsley story. Some say love and basketball don't mix, but we'll soon find out.

Martha

ALWAYS My BABY

MARTHA KENNERSON

HARLEQUIN® KIMANI™ ROMANCE

Recycling programs
for this product may
not exist in your area.

ISBN-13: 978-0-373-86499-7

Always My Baby

Copyright © 2017 by Martha Kennerson

HARLEQUIN®
www.Harlequin.com

Printed in U.S.A.

Martha Kennerson's love of reading and writing is a significant part of who she is, and she uses both to create the kinds of stories that touch your heart. Martha lives with her family in League City, Texas, and believes her current blessings are only matched by the struggle it took to achieve such happiness. To find out more about Martha and her journey, check out her website at marthakennerson.com.

Books by Martha Kennerson

Harlequin Kimani Romance

Visit the Author Profile page
at Harlequin.com for more titles.

I'd like to dedicate this story to all my male readers
who reached out and expressed their gratitude and
appreciation for the way I construct my heroes.

Acknowledgments
I'd like to thank my friend and agent, Lissa,
for giving me the encouragement and guidance needed
to make my dreams come true.

Chapter 1

Alexander Kingsley Jr. stood barefoot in his dimly lit, downtown Houston high-rise office, staring out of his wall of windows. The usually immaculately dressed COO of Kingsley Oil and Gas, his family's multibillion-dollar conglomerate, wore black jeans and a black T-shirt, clothes that reflected his mood. Alexander held a glass of single malt whiskey low at his side as he watched the rain blanket the dark city.

The eldest son of the wealthy Creole and African American Kingsley family and heir apparent to take over as the company's CEO upon his mother's retirement, he was used to carrying the weight of his company's decisions, and the consequences associated with those decisions, on his shoulders, yet this new threat had him questioning his next move. Alexander heard his door open and grimaced. *This won't be pretty.*

"Really, Alexander? You summoned me back to the office on a Friday night…again. And in the rain at that. This had better be important."

"Come in, China," Alexander ordered, his tone flat as he kept his back to her. "Fix yourself a drink. You're going to need it."

China Edwards, Alexander's beautiful best friend, was an environmental attorney whom Alexander thought of as basically a female version of himself. Her sharp mind, quick wit and photographic memory made China's position as in-house counsel for Kingsley Oil and Gas vital to the ongoing success of their company.

Alexander could hear the annoyance in her voice. He picked up a small framed photo of the two of them, taken on the day of their law school graduation. The corner of his mouth rose. "Remember that promise we made each other the day we graduated?"

China sighed, tossed her Chloé handbag on the sectional sofa placed in Alexander's lounge, an area attached to his office but separated by a collapsible wall. "Which one?" she asked, making her way through the lounge, passing a wood and granite-topped coffee table to get to the matching bar. She picked up the bottle, read the label and said, "Nikka Forty…very nice. This must be big when you're reaching for the good whiskey."

Alexander turned to face China, and his eyes widened at the sight before him. He'd always thought she was gorgeous but something was different about tonight. China's long, curly brown hair was pulled back off her face into a high ponytail, showcasing her stunning warm ivory skin tone. She wore a black sequined shorts set with gold stiletto heels that seemed to extend her legs. "Damn!" Even in his current state of annoyance Alexander's body responded to the beauty of his best friend. Alexander had been finding it more and more difficult to keep his attraction for China under control, and tonight wasn't helping his case.

"What?" China questioned, looking down at herself. "Why are you looking at me like that?" She leaned against the bar.

"Like what?" His eyes looked their fill at her body and his voice took on a husky tone.

"Like that...like I'm one of those women you 'date,'" she stated, using air quotes to emphasize the point that she didn't think he actually did anything beyond sleeping with any of them.

China bent back her left leg and released her heel from her shoe's strap. She removed one shoe, then the other, tossing them both to the side, which dropped her to her normal height of five feet five inches. China sipped her drink as she took a seat in an oversized round chair that sat between Alexander's desk and the bar.

"I'm not." Alexander broke eye contact and returned the photo to its resting place on the long credenza that had been positioned behind his desk. *Get a grip, man; this is China.* He turned back and met her intense gaze.

"Sure you are," she alleged before taking another drink from her glass.

"Where are you coming from, dressed like that, anyway?" His nose wrinkled.

"Not that it's any of your business, but my date took me dancing." China smiled as though she'd just remembered something pleasant.

Alexander felt like he'd been hit with a sharp object. "Date...you went on a date?"

China rolled her eyes skyward. "Yes, Alexander, it happens."

"Since when?"

"Since now." China's phone beeped indicating that she

had an incoming text. She got up and went to where her purse had landed, retrieved the phone and read the text. China laughed before typing out a response. She put her purse and phone on the coffee table and returned to the chair. "Why did you summon me back here at ten o'clock at night?" she reiterated.

"Do you remember the promise?"

She grinned. "Which one?"

"The one where we said we'd always be there for each other, no matter what."

"Well, let's see." She tapped her temple twice before letting her index finger rest on the side of her head. "We've been best friends since law school. We have dinner together every month, which you insist on cooking. You drag me to every formal function *you're* invited to in order to keep gold digging women away and I've worked for you and your family for the past seven years." She dropped her hand. "I'd say we had that, 'I'll always have your back' phase of our relationship covered."

Alexander smiled and scratched his beard with his left hand.

"What's going on, Alex?"

Alexander's sex throbbed at the sound of China using the shortened version of his name that only she was allowed to use. It was something special just between the two of them. "The government is coming for us."

China sighed and dismissed his concern with a wave of her hand. "Again…"

"Yes, but this time they may have a case."

China sat up straight in her chair. "What do you mean?"

"The Environmental Protection Agency claims to have proof that we disposed of our gas cylinders illegally and to the detriment of the environment. They're opening an official investigation and announcing it Monday morning," he explained.

"That's not possible," she declared.

"Apparently it is." He tossed back the rest of his drink and moved over to the bar to pour himself more. He picked up the bottle and showed it to China. "Another?"

"Sure." She swiveled her chair around and reached for her glass, stretching across the chair, offering Alexander a nice view of her outstretched legs and round behind. "How did you find this out?" China offered him her glass.

"My mother has some very expensive and well-placed sources," he said, pouring the golden substance into her glass.

"Don't I know it? We can't do anything about it until we know what they have, which could take a few weeks after I put in a request for discovery," she reminded him.

Alexander took a drink and said, "Actually—"

"Actually what?" Her brows knit together.

"We'll have a copy of what they have Monday," Alexander promised.

"EPA investigations are secret, even the preliminary ones. What did you do?" China asked, her eyes narrowed.

"Remember that promise," he said, giving her a sheepish grin.

"What…did…you…do?"

"*I* didn't do anything. My mother, on the other hand, made arrangements for us to get a sneak peek at everything the government has."

China shook her head slowly. "Why am I not surprised?" She tossed back her drink.

"Because you know my mother." Alexander folded his body onto his extra-wide and extra-long sectional. He stretched out his long legs and laid his head against the sofa's high, round back. "The rain's really coming down now," Alexander observed.

"Yes, it is. It looks like we'll be here a minute. Just another late night at the office, thanks to you."

"Hey, we have alcohol and snacks," Alexander offered.

"There is that." Her sarcasm came through loud and clear.

China rose from the chair and went to join Alexander on the daybed portion of the sectional. She curled up, pulled down the decorative throw that was hanging across the back of the sofa and covered her legs. China laid her head against one of the large pillows.

"You know we didn't do anything wrong, right? Whatever this is about, we will handle it." China raised her head slightly and said, "The right way." She gave him a knowing look.

Alexander laughed and turned toward China. "Why didn't you tell me you had a new man?"

"You don't tell me about every woman you sleep with." China laid her head back down.

Alexander's heart sank and his breath caught in his throat. He didn't understand why. China had never been his, so why did he suddenly feel a sense of betrayal? "Oh, it's like that?" His left eyebrow rose.

China pushed out a breath. "No, it's not. This was only our second date and it got cut short thanks to another one of *your* emergencies…nonemergency call," she said, closing her eyes.

Alexander had refused to explore why lately he found himself having emergencies that required China's immediate attention whenever she was out on dates. "Oh…sorry."

"No, you're not," she said, keeping her eyes closed.

No, I'm not. Alexander watched the rise and fall of China's chest with each slow breath she took. He marveled at the curve between her neck and shoulder, and the delicate way her hands lay at her sides. Alexander had always been attracted to China, but for the sake of their friendship, he'd buried his attraction and complicated feelings for his best friend. He hadn't always had the best track record when it came to his relationships with women. Alexander never wanted to do anything that would jeopardize their friendship; however, his overwhelming feelings now had him…questioning that wisdom.

"China," Alexander whispered.

It was a sound that sent a warm, familiar tingling throughout her body. "Yes…" China could feel the warmth of Alexander's breath on her face and her body began to respond in ways that it shouldn't.

"You 'sleep?"

"Maybe." China slowly opened her eyes to Alexander's face inches from hers.

"Can I ask you something?" Alexander pushed a strand of loose hair behind her ear before running the back of his right index finger slowly down the side of her face, and China's nipples instantly hardened.

What the hell is wrong with you, girl? This is Alexander. "Of course." *But you really need to stop touching me.*

"Have you ever wondered what it would be like?" Alexander held her gaze as he imprisoned her chin with his thumb and index finger. "Between the two of us."

China blinked to make sure she wasn't dreaming. After all, this was her best friend talking. The one person she trusted above all others. The only man whose friendship she cherished more than any sexual desire that she may have had for him. "Yes, but…"

Alexander captured China's mouth in a mind-melting kiss that she responded to with just as much fervor. "I want

you," he proclaimed, coming up for air. Alexander ran his
tongue across her lips, removed her hair clip and buried
his fingers in her hair. He slid his tongue across her jaw
and down her neck.

China's body begged for surrender while her mind was
trying to fight through the thick fog of her unrelenting desire. *What the hell are you doing? This is Alexander. He's
a brilliant businessman and the best friend you've ever
had but when it comes to making long-term commitments
to women he's just not that guy.* "I…I'm not…"

Alexander raised his head, looked into her eyes and
said, "I'll stop if you want me to." His eyes roamed her
face. "Please don't want me to."

"I just don't want to ruin things between us," she whispered before leaning forward, kissing him gently on the
lips. "But I can't seem to stop touching you, either."

"It won't. I promise." Alexander kissed her on the corner of her mouth. "And please don't stop touching me."

China had always wondered what it would be like to
make love with Alexander…to be devoured by him. The
thought of spending one rainy night together seemed harm-
less, especially with the new direction that her life would
soon be taking. It was a direction she knew Alexander
would support but never agree with. Now might be the
only time she could satisfy her curiosity without lasting
repercussions. China confined Alexander's face between
her hands and kissed him as though it would be her last
opportunity. They kissed each other with urgency, as if
each was afraid the other would change their mind.

Clothes were ripped off and thrown across the room.
Alexander retrieved a condom from a hidden compartment inside the drawer of his coffee table. China threw
her head back and laughed at the move. "Well, it is Friday
night and you were a Boy Scout."

"What?" Alexander frowned.

"Always being prepared…and you even have creative hiding places for your personal items, too," she teased.

Alexander silenced her with another heart-piercing kiss. He ran his nose and lips along the edge of her cheek and down the side of her neck to her shoulder. Alexander slowly kissed his way down the valley of her breasts to her left nipple, where he sucked and pulled as if she was providing him with the sweetest nectar.

China arched her back and moaned, "Yes, Alex…yes."

Within seconds Alexander had rolled the condom on, had China's left leg over his shoulder and her right hooked around his waist, and he was buried deep inside of her. The initial thrust of his hips sent China's body into a crazed frenzy. She had never felt so reckless and complete all at the same time, and she loved every moment of it. The idea of maintaining her celibacy was quickly fading to the background.

Their sexual roller-coaster ride was something China had never experienced before. Alexander made sure they both enjoyed every peak and valley before they took that last intense dive over the edge. They both lay naked, flat on their backs across the daybed, trying to catch their breath.

"That was—"

"Cr… Crazy!" China said between gulps of air.

"Exhilarating," he corrected, turning toward her. "Who knew you were so flexible?"

China turned her head toward him. "You should have. How many gymnastic competitions did you come see me in?"

"Yeah, but that was years ago. I had no idea you could still do the splits, and in so many different ways, too."

China laughed and covered her face with both hands. "Shut up."

"I'll be right back." Alexander made his way to the bathroom.

China dropped her hands. "Girl, what in the hell did you just do? You can't even blame it on the alcohol," she said to herself, giggling.

Alexander returned and scooped China up into his arms. "What are you doing?" she asked, loving the feel of his sweaty skin against her own.

"Shower time." Alexander carried China into the bathroom, where they showered and made love again. After helping China dry off, Alexander offered her one of his dress shirts that he kept at the office. She slipped it on and they returned to the daybed where they lay snuggling, watching the rain and falling asleep in each other's arms.

Chapter 2

China woke to the sound of her cell phone beeping. She was naked and lying on top of a sound-asleep Alexander. At some point in the night they had made love again, but this time decided to forgo showering or clothes. Making love with Alexander had been better than China had ever imagined. His powerful yet gentle touch had awakened emotions that she knew she had to bring under control. China eased off Alexander, reached for his dress shirt that was now on the floor and quickly wrapped her body in it.

The automatic shades on Alexander's windows had kicked in, preventing the morning sunlight from shining completely through the room. China picked up her phone, read the message and moved over to the conference table that sat on the other side of Alexander's large mahogany desk. She hit her phone's redial button and waited for the call to connect.

"Good morning, Jackson."

Jackson Weatherly, a successful pediatric surgeon from a wealthy family of physicians, was China's date from the previous night.

"You okay? I got worried when I didn't hear back from you," he stated, his voice full of concern.

"I'm fine," she said, not quite sure if she really believed that. "Things got a little crazy here last night."

"You're still at the office?" Jackson's voice raised an octave.

"Yes."

"Wow, talk about dedication," he replied.

"That's one way of putting it." China covered her eyes with her left hand and shook her head.

"How about I come pick you up and take you out for breakfast?"

"Not today, Jackson. I have some loose ends I need to tie up here." China knew that no matter how wonderful their night may have been, giving in to her desires for Alexander had been a mistake. He wasn't prepared to give her the one thing she so desperately wanted: a child. "How about brunch tomorrow?"

"Sunday it is. I'll pick you up at eleven," he promised.

"See you then." China ended the call, sensing she was no longer alone.

"A loose end, am I?" a deep baritone voice asked.

China turned to find a naked and erect Alexander standing with his arms folded, glaring down at her. She quickly diverted her eyes, but her body was already responding to the sight. No matter how hard she tried, China knew she couldn't hide her physical response to the man who'd provided her with an unendurable amount of pleasure all night.

"Put some clothes on, Alexander." China shifted in her

seat, trying to relieve the instant pressure rising between her legs.

Alexander's expression dulled. "Oh, it's Alexander now. Last night it was *yes, Alex...right there, Alex...how do you like this, Alex?*" He turned like a defiant child forced to follow his parents' orders. Alexander reached for his pants and quickly slipped them on.

"That was last night, which was—"

"Don't you dare say it was a mistake," he said to the back of her head.

China placed her phone on the table, turned and met Alexander's angry leer. She could almost see the fury radiating from his body. China stood, walked over to him and placed both hands on his chest. She stared up into his eyes and said, "No, it wasn't a mistake. Last night was curiosity being explored. It was a magnificent experience that's over and can't happen again. We're friends, remember?"

Alexander dropped his arms, placed his left hand over hers and sighed. "Always."

"Good." She pulled her hands free. "Now finish getting dressed and give me a ride home."

"You really don't think we should even talk about last night?" His forehead puckered. "Maybe see where this thing could lead."

"No. One night doesn't change the people we are... what we want. Our friendship works because we don't try to push our individual needs and wants onto each other," China reminded him.

"That's because for years our needs and wants have always been in sync."

China twisted her neck and raised her left eyebrow. "*Almost* all of our needs."

"You mean the kid thing." Alexander placed his hands in his pants pockets.

"Yes, the kid thing. I want them and I'm building my life around having them, and you're indifferent on the subject. That alone prevents us from going any further than last night." China placed her right hand on her hip. "You can wait until whenever to have children. Women aren't so lucky. I know firsthand what it's like to have an older parent and I won't do that to my child...hopefully children."

China had been raised by a single mother in the military, and while she'd loved the travel and different adventures they got to experience, having an older mother with sensitive, fair Irish skin prone to wrinkles had made things uncomfortable for China growing up; people assumed that her mother was her grandmother. Her mother's love of the sun hadn't helped the situation, either. She'd died from an aggressive form of skin cancer before China's twenty-first birthday.

"You're barely twenty-nine years old, China, and you sound like you're on some deadline," he declared, his apathy on the subject clear.

I am. "I need someone who's of the same mindset as me when it comes to having children, and I think I may have found someone." China started gathering up her clothes.

"Have you, now?"

"I'm not discussing this with you right now, Alexander." Between thoughts of her mother, China's own desperate need to create a family and dealing with feelings that being with Alexander unleashed, the last thing China wanted was for Alexander to see her break down; his kind heart and big strong shoulders would be hard to resist. She was drowning in emotions and needed space to pull herself together. China disappeared into the bathroom.

Alexander watched China retreat to his private bathroom. "Dammit," he said, as he pounded his right fist into his left hand. Even after a rambunctious night of lovemaking with China, Alexander's body still craved her unlike any other woman he'd had. He wasn't sure what this thing between them was, but he was determined to figure it out. He was not going to just give up. Alexander was moving toward the bathroom when he heard his office door open. He turned just in time to see his family's matriarchs cross the threshold. Watching China walk away from him while his mother and aunt walked toward him as he stood in his office shirtless had Alexander wondering if the last couple of minutes had been a nightmare.

Victoria Langston Kingsley and Elizabeth Langston Kingsley, Alexander's mother and aunt, had inherited their father's floundering corporation, and with the help of their husbands—brothers Alexander and Harrison Kingsley— the sisters turned their struggling company into one of the most successful privately held oil and natural gas companies in the country.

"I told you he'd be here," Victoria proudly declared, entering the office wearing a gray-and-white St. John suit with gray pumps. She wore a small amount of makeup and her hair was pulled back in a tight, conservative bun. Victoria was athletically built and looked nowhere near her fifty-plus years. She was carrying a white cardboard box with a large envelope on its top, placing it on the desk before Alexander could offer his assistance. "In a crisis, where else would he be?"

"That you did, sister dear. Like mother, like son," Elizabeth said, brushing a long, curly strand of hair behind her ear and looking just as young and fit as her sister.

"Mother…Aunt Elizabeth, what are you doing here?" Alexander asked, briefly looking over his shoulder and grabbing his T-shirt as he moved into his office out of the lounge. He pulled the shirt over his head before kissing his mother on the cheek.

"Well, good morning to you, too," Victoria replied, tilting her head.

Alexander placed his right hand over his heart. "My apologies. Good morning, ladies."

"Better!" Victoria said, her mouth set firm.

"Good morning, nephew. You do realize that you have a striking home, right? Try staying in it more often," his aunt advised before pulling Alexander into her arms for a hug.

"I'll keep that in mind," Alexander promised, stepping out of her arms. "Don't you both look lovely this morning."

"I look lovely." Victoria pointed to herself. "In that long, flower-print dress, with its giant matching hat that's in the car, Liz looks like a painting."

"A Rembrandt," Elizabeth snapped back before taking a seat at the conference table.

"More like a Warhol," Victoria countered.

Alexander laughed. "What brings you two here on a Saturday morning?"

"If you'd checked your messages you'd have seen I've been trying to reach you," Victoria explained.

Alexander retrieved his phone from his desk. "What's so important that it couldn't wait until I got back to you?"

"Or at least until after our board meeting this morning," Elizabeth added, checking her watch.

"Board meeting?" Alexander's eyes danced between his mother and aunt.

"At the Children's Museum," Victoria clarified.

"Yes, of course. You did mention that," he said, nodding.

"Son, you seem to forget anything I say that's even remotely related to children. You automatically assume it would lead me to requesting grandchildren."

"That's because it usually does," Elizabeth said as she examined the nails on her outstretched hand. "Do you think this lime-green polish is too much?"

"For you, no," Victoria replied.

Alexander stifled his laugh. "Where was I?" Victoria asked to no one in particular. "Oh, yes, grandchildren."

Alexander ran both hands down his face. "Not you, too." Alexander was in no mood to deal with another one of his mother's lectures on the importance of him having heirs, especially with China in the next room thinking basically the same thing, only about herself.

"Not me, too…what?" Victoria frowned at Alexander.

"Never mind. I assume all this is for me," he said, gesturing with his head toward the box and envelope as he leaned against his desk.

"Yes, but Alexander, why *did* you stay here last night?" Victoria glanced around the room. "I know this is like a second home, but really, son, how can you get any rest on that thing?" Victoria questioned, pointing at his sectional sofa.

China's face, her body and the smell of her skin flooded his mind. Alexander felt his body start to stir and he quickly moved away from his mother and took a seat behind his desk. "It's fine, Mother. What's in the box?"

"My source came through early," she said, smiling and handing him the envelope. "You might want to call China. She'll need to help us on this one."

"I already did. We're just waiting for this." He tapped the envelope.

Elizabeth rose and ran her hand down the front of her dress. "Now that that's done…"

"I could stay and go over all of this with you and China," Victoria offered.

"No, you can't," Elizabeth chastised. "We have other pressing business to attend to."

Victoria turned and faced Elizabeth. "Sister dear, this is our company we're talking about."

"And we have four of our six extremely intelligent and very capable children helping us run it, too." Elizabeth went and stood next to her sister. "Children that you trained, I might add, all being led by your handsome husband's clone. Our company is in excellent hands."

Victoria released a quick breath. "You're right." She turned and faced Alexander. "I've done my part...now you do your job, son. Find out what the hell is going on and put a stop to it. Quickly!"

"I'll do my best."

"I don't expect anything less." Victoria picked up her purse and followed her sister to the door.

Alexander heard his aunt ask his mother, "Did you see it?"

"Of course I did." Both sisters laughed, closing the door behind them.

Alexander dropped his head and sighed. "You can come out now," he called, breaking the seal on the envelope with a letter opener from his desk.

"Victoria's something else," China said, taking a seat on the edge of the high-backed chair in front of Alexander's desk.

"Yes, she is." Alexander marveled at China. He always thought she was a ravishing woman, but never more than when she was in such a relaxed state, free of makeup and with her hair down, still wet from the shower.

China was wearing last night's clothes and had a pair of Alexander's socks on her feet. "So, what do we have here?"

"I was just about to find out." Alexander slid the contents of the envelope onto his desk to find several smaller ones, a set of legal documents and three flash drives. He opened the box to find several binders and a number of different-colored folders.

China reached for the legal documents and began flipping through the pages, reading each word with blinding speed. "We're going to need to bring everybody in on this," she said, frowning. "And I mean everyone."

"Why? What is it?" Alexander got up, walked around his desk and came to stand next to China, reading over her shoulder. He had to fight hard to focus. His shampoo, which China had used, mixed with her own sweet scent, was assaulting his senses, sending his hormones into overdrive.

"In a nutshell, the government alleges that we systematically and purposely misled the EPA with our ongoing practice to dispose of gas cylinders. They state that we did so in order to save money."

"That's ridiculous. We submitted our disposal plans for approval, which we received, and we've been following them ever since." Alexander's jaw tightened.

China shrugged and shook her head. "They claim to have proof that we submitted false plans in order to get the approval, then changed the procedures to save money. They claim to have a witness and documentation to this change, a whistle-blower, so to speak."

"A whistle-blower? There's nothing to blow," he said, slamming his palm against his desk.

"Stay calm, Alexander," she said, as she continued to examine the papers on his desk.

"We pay *you* to stay calm." Alexander returned to his desk and powered up his computer. "Let's see what's on these flash drives."

China looked around the room. "Where's my phone?"

"It's on the conference table. By the way, they know you were here."

"Who?" she asked, rising to go collect her phone.

"Mom and Aunt Liz."

China's face was marred by confusion. "How?"

Alexander laughed at the shocked look on China's face. "They saw your phone. Not many people have a pink diamond-encrusted phone case exactly like the one that they had specifically designed for you and gave to you."

"Oh, no…" China dropped her face into both hands, and her hair fell forward.

Alexander had to force himself to concentrate on the problem at hand, when all he really wanted to do was lower her hands, brush China's hair to the side and kiss her senseless. "Don't worry about it. I'm sure they figured it was a business-related visit," he said, trying to sound as convincing as possible.

"Yeah, right, and how do I explain not coming out and greeting them like always?" China flopped back down in the chair and started dialing her phone.

"Who are you calling?"

"Joyce. We need her here and I want her to stop by my house and bring me a change of clothes."

Joyce was China's legal assistant and good friend.

"Clothes?"

"Yes, clothes, pants, a shirt and underwear—"

"Underwear." Alexander smirked.

China rolled her eyes. "Stop it. I'm not going commando the rest of the day."

Alexander felt his sex spring to life and was relieved that he was sitting. He reached for his desk phone. "I guess I'll call in the rest of the cavalry. They won't be happy about us interrupting their Saturday."

"Too bad. It's either us or your mother."

"Good point," he agreed just as his computer beeped and several documents popped up on both of Alexander's screens. He stared in disbelief.

China leaned over the desk to get a better view of what had captured his attention. "Call Morgan…" she ordered.

Alexander shook his head. "I don't know anything about this—"

"Call your brother…right now," China said, her voice icy and emotionless.

Chapter 3

China sat at the conference table mulling over all the papers that lay in front of her, her face contorted. "I don't understand any of this." She picked up a spiral booklet with the word *Approved* stamped in red across its cover. "This is the procedure manual that was submitted."

"It's also the exact procedure we put in place," Morgan confirmed, standing with his feet apart and arms folded across his chest.

Morgan Kingsley, the ruggedly handsome and athletically built second eldest of the Kingsley boys, was vice president of field operations for their company and was quickly running out of patience with the mess they found themselves in. "There is no way in hell these procedures could have been changed without our approval or my direct knowledge and supervision," he explained, his mouth set in a hard line.

"Dammit." Alexander slammed his fist against the conference room table. "I didn't sign off on any changes, and I certainly didn't authorize any money transfers. Why would I jeopardize everything to save a few bucks?" Alexander asked the flabbergasted room.

"We know," everyone said in unison.

"Well, according to the whistle-blower's statement and these financial records—" Brice Kingsley, Alexander and Morgan's younger brother and the company's CFO, held up a ledger and a spreadsheet "—we've saved more than just a few bucks."

"If that's the case, where the hell is all the money?" Alexander asked.

"Good question. My financial records are on point and all of our audits have been clean," Brice informed them confidently.

"Everyone just calm down," China murmured, keeping her eyes on the pages of the procedures manual.

Alexander frowned at China. "Calm down? This is our reputation at risk...my reputation. We're talking about claims that could turn into charges if we can't provide evidence that not only proves whoever this whistle-blower is lied, but that everything we've done is legal and above reproach."

China rose and moved over to where Alexander stood. She looked up at him, placed her right hand over his heart and said, "You pay me to worry...remember, I got this."

Alexander's shoulders dropped. "What do you have in mind?"

"Yeah, what *do* you have in mind, China?" Morgan echoed.

China turned and faced all three brothers. "We're going to let the whistle-blower tell us where, why and how." The corner of her mouth rose slowly.

"Wait, you know who this person is?" Brice asked, frowning.

"We all do," she said confidently.

"What?" the brothers cried out.

China moved back to the table and gestured with her hands at all the documents that lay spread out over the conference table. "All of this information was provided by someone we know or came in contact with. What we have to do is go through every inch of this material and figure out who it could be. We'll make a list—"

"A list?" Brice asked.

China leaned across the table and selected one of the statements that had been provided. She flipped through the pages. "Here." She tapped the page with her index finger. "It says the whistle-blower was present doing an operations meeting in January with you, Morgan." She looked up from the document, her eyes lasering in on his confused look . "That you were discussing the various ways to save money in the area of waste disposal. Did any such meeting occur?"

"Yes, but nothing came up about changing the way we handle gas cylinders," Morgan assured her.

"Do you remember who all was in the room?" she inquired, dropping the document on the table.

"Everyone," Morgan said.

"What do you mean?" China asked.

"It was our first meeting of the year." Morgan placed his hands in his pockets. "There were over three hundred people in attendance."

"Any senior-level management executives?" China questioned.

"Not really?" He shrugged and shook his head.

"Think, man," Alexander ordered; his voice rose.

"I am!" Morgan responded, with an equal amount of

force in his voice. He pulled his hands free and started rubbing them together as he started pacing the room. "Mom was there, along with my three lead foremen, Danny, Roger and the new guy, Big Usher."

"Big Usher?" China asked, frowning.

"Yeah, he's the new junior assistant. We hired him six months ago," Morgan explained, stopping his movement.

"Just about the time the whistle-blower started providing information to the government," China concluded.

"Usher's a good kid…he's not the whistle-blower. Besides, there's nothing to blow," Morgan reiterated.

"Who else was there?" China reached for a bottle of water.

"I can't think of everyone. I don't have your photographic memory, China."

China laughed. "That's for what I read, but you don't need one. We can just pull the minutes from the meeting." China picked up her phone and pulled down the recorder app, tapped it on and said, "Have the January operations notes pulled." She sat the phone down. "This is the process we'll have to follow with all of this information."

"Mom's contact really was efficient in pulling all this together," Brice said.

Alexander raised his left eyebrow. "Are you really surprised?"

"Not at all." Brice shook his head.

"What do we do after we get this list together?" Morgan asked.

"We go fishing," Alexander replied. "Once we have our list of targets, we divide and conquer. Figure out who's trying to sabotage us."

"And?" Brice questioned, frowning. His eyes cut to Morgan, who stood with a menacing look on his face.

"Then you let me do my job," China said, glaring at

all three brothers. The last thing she needed was for them to take matters into their own hands. "In the meantime, I'll work up our initial response to the complaint, which is basically a clear and precise denial. We have forty-five days to submit it. Hopefully we'll figure out what's really going on, too, sooner than later."

"What if we don't know what happened in forty-five days?" Morgan asked.

"We have a hundred and twenty days from the initial response to file our final one that will either substantiate our denial, as long as we provide solid evidence to back up our claim, or we can request an administrative oversight ruling."

"An administrative oversight ruling…what the hell is that?" Alexander's eyebrows stood at attention.

"It's the EPA's way of giving some companies an out without having to admit guilt to anything. It's like saying we simply made a mistake. But…" China raised her right index finger. "Companies still must pay fines and clean-up expenses if necessary, and their reputations usually take a pretty big hit and…"

"And what?" Alexander asked.

"Someone usually has to resign," China said, staring into Alexander's eyes. She could see past the bluster of his anger to his vulnerability, and all she wanted to do was help him find his place of calm. In that moment, China's body was reminding her that what was happening between them was much more than she'd ever expected.

"But everyone stays out of jail, right?" Brice asked, his whole face lit up.

"Right." China smirked.

"There was no damn administrative oversight. It didn't happen and I certainly didn't steal from my own damn company," Alexander insisted. She could almost see the anger radiating from his body.

"Of course not, but something happened, Alexander. We just have to prove what that was and that we're innocent of any wrongdoing," China explained.

"If we can." Alexander ran his right hand through his hair.

"*When* we do, they'll close the case and issue a letter clearing us," China promised.

"If not?" Morgan questioned, pulling out his cell phone to silence the ringing.

"Things get a lot more complicated. The courts get involved," China explained.

"What do we do about the media explosion that's coming? Life is going to get really crazy…very quickly," Morgan warned.

"It's not like we're not used to the attention," Brice reminded him, offering a nonchalant shrug.

"True, but Mom usually nips it in the bud before things get out of hand. She won't be able to stop this runaway train," Alexander said, shaking his head.

"Yeah, the EPA thinks they've got us by the balls, so they'll turn up the heat big-time." Morgan cracked the knuckles of both his hands. "We have to give KJ and Travis a heads-up."

Keylan James Kingsley, or KJ, was Victoria's youngest son and a professional basketball player in the NBA. Travis Kingsley, the youngest child of Elizabeth, was a successful cattle rancher who preferred a private existence and had little to do with their family's business.

"Travis is really going to love this," Brice said mockingly.

"We'll deal with that next week. Right now, let's start going through all this material that Victoria bought…I mean, *brought* for us to review." China's sarcasm wasn't lost on anyone as she started distributing the different stacks of paper.

"There go my dinner plans," Morgan said, taking a seat at the conference table.

"Dinner? We'll be lucky to get through all of this before the sun rises Monday morning," Brice countered, picking up a stack of papers.

China took the seat offered by Alexander. His hands grazed her arms and a warm shiver ran down her spine. "Th-thank you."

"Anytime," he said, in a tone that garnered his brothers' attention. He met their stares. "What?"

"Nothing," both brothers said in unison, passing a look between them.

China kept her eyes on the documents in front of her. The last thing she needed was for the other Kingsley men to figure out something was different between her and Alexander.

"Let's get to work, gentlemen," China ordered.

Alexander sat at his desk reading over the list of names he'd been given to follow up on. After a painful two-day review of documents accusing him and their company of malicious malfeasance, Alexander didn't feel any more confident in their plan to find the culprit behind the unsubstantiated accusations. He was reaching for his coffee cup when he heard his office door being opened. Alexander looked up to see his cousin Kristen almost bounce into the room.

Kristen, Elizabeth's eldest child, was vice president of general operations and in line to take over Alexander's role as COO upon his promotion to CEO.

"Good morning, Alexander," Kristen called out cheerfully as she entered his office, holding an electronic tablet in one hand and a large travel mug for her coffee in the other. The black-and-white Chanel suit that covered her petite body was much like something his mother would wear, and her mother would revolt against, and it made him smile.

Alexander turned and faced his computer. "Kristen, you really should cut down on the caffeine."

She took a seat in front of his desk and rested her cup on its corner. "And *you*, my dear cousin, really should focus on the problem at hand. Sorry I'm late. I got here as fast as I could."

"Late for what?" he asked, his brow puckered as he tapped the keys of his computer.

"Don't tell me you didn't get my message."

The night before, Kristen had left Alexander a twenty-minute-long voice mail outlining her plans for a press conference and the message she felt they needed to convey. She'd even followed that up with a detailed email.

"I got it," he assured her.

"Good, because we really need to get out in front of the EPA's announcement." Kristen took a sip from her cup.

"I guess…"

"You *guess*." Kristen tilted her head slightly and her nose crinkled. "I know you've been working nonstop on this thing for the last forty-eight hours, but you've got to pull it together before you and China go in front of those cameras for the press conference."

Alexander's mind flashed back to the last time he and China had come together, literally. He thought back to the way she looked, how she smelled and the way she tasted. "Alexander… Alexander," Kristen said, knocking on his desk with her hand.

"What…?"

"You okay?" she questioned. "I lost you there for a minute."

"I'm good…just tired." He rubbed his eyes. "I'll be fine. Especially with China by my side," he murmured, turning his attention back to the computer screen.

"What was that?" Kristen's eyebrows came together and she sat forward in her chair. "What's going on?"

"What do you mean?" Alexander kept his eyes on the screen.

"With you and China. Something happen I should know about?"

Definitely not. "Like what?"

"Anything that could be picked up by the cameras. A disagreement on how the investigation is being handled, maybe," she suggested.

Alexander turned his head and met his cousin's gaze. "Not at all. We're all on the same page in that regard."

"Good, because even the slightest hint of a crack in our united front will be picked up on by those media vultures."

"China and I will be fine…just like always," he pledged.

"Great. Now let's go over your statement," she said, powering up her tablet.

Alexander pushed out a breath. Before he could reply, there was a knock on the door just before it slowly opened. His longtime assistant, Tammy, stood in the doorway. "Excuse me, Alexander. China asked me to tell you that she'll meet you at the press conference. She had to step out for a while."

Alexander frowned. "Step out." He checked his watch. "Did she say where she was going?"

"She went out for an early lunch," Tammy explained.

"That's fine. Thanks, Tammy."

"No problem. By the way, that stewardess chick keeps

calling for you. I guess she didn't get the memo that once it's over it's over and calling me won't help."

"They prefer 'flight attendant,' and I'll take care of it."

Kristen narrowed her eyes. "Okay…spill. What's going on, Alexander?"

Alexander knew how hard it was to get anything past the Kingsley women, but he certainly was going to try. The last thing he needed was for his cousin to start digging into his personal business. "I have no idea what you're talking about. Don't you have a press conference you need to co-ordinate or something?"

"Avoidance. That's something this family's good at. Just remember what I said about the press picking up on anything out of the ordinary." Kristen rose, collected her things and left the office.

"Sleeping with China is definitely out of the ordinary," he said, slouching back in his chair, wishing he had another chance to do even more out of the ordinary things with China.

Chapter 4

"Thanks again for meeting me. I wasn't sure you would want to after—"

"After you ended our date early Friday night and canceled our brunch date yesterday," Jackson reminded her, offering up a teasing smile.

China nodded as she reached for her glass of water and took a sip. She appreciated the handsome, brown-skinned pediatric surgeon for being so patient with her, but unfortunately her night with Alexander had started to cloud her feelings; China was beginning to question her decision. The past weekend was just one more example of how important it was to have her own family, especially in times of crisis. No family was better at standing strong together when they thought they were being attacked than the Kingsleys. While China's secret desire was to have that experience with Alexander, she knew that wasn't something he wanted.

"Yes, basically, and I wouldn't blame you if you had canceled," she said.

Jackson trained his green eyes on her as he signaled for the waiter. "Don't be ridiculous. Lunch with you has brightened up my Monday. We're both very busy people, which is why we signed up with More Than Just Dating in the first place."

More Than Just Dating was an exclusive matchmaking agency that specialized in setting up individuals of discerning taste and sizable wealth who either wanted to get married or become parents through donations, sperm or egg.

A tall male waiter approached the table. "Good evening, I'm Al. Can I get you something to drink?" he asked, handing them both menus.

"Yes, please. Can you bring us two Arnold Palmers?" Jackson asked.

"Right away, sir."

"How did you know I like Arnold Palmers?" Her forehead crinkled.

"Your profile questionnaire, remember?" he said, laughing. "After having to answer all those questions on that assessment myself, I was certainly going to read everyone else's answers."

"That really was some questionnaire," she agreed, smiling. *I would've loved to hear Alexander's opinion on some of those questions. He would've laughed his head off. Focus, China. This is about you and Jackson...not Alexander.*

"What is it about that questionnaire that's making you smile in such a way?" Jackson asked, as the corner of his mouth rose slightly.

The waiter returned with their drinks, placing a glass in front of each of them. "Are you ready to order?"

"Yes," Jackson replied quickly. "Do you mind if I…"

"Not at all," China said, impressed by his initiative and grateful for the subject change.

"We'll have two house salads with grilled chicken, and please have the special house dressing placed on the side."

"Yes, sir." The waiter collected the menus before leaving.

China reached for her glass. "Let me guess, the questionnaire?"

"Yes." Jackson picked up his tea and raised the glass skyward. "To hopefully an uninterrupted lunch."

China smiled and touched her glass against his. "One can always hope," she murmured before taking a drink.

Jackson placed his glass down and said, "So, what was that pretty smile a moment ago all about?"

Alexander's face, his body and all of the intimate things that they had done flooded her mind. China dropped her eyes in hopes of hiding emotions she had no control of, it seemed, when it came to Alexander. "What makes you think there's more to it?"

"Because that smile lit up your eyes, like now." Jackson leaned forward as though he was about to share some top-secret information that he didn't want others to hear. "I'd like to think I've done a few things that evoked that kind of response in you."

Damn you, Alexander. China reached for her napkin and laid it across her lap. "It's nothing…really. It's just this whole process is taking some getting used to, that's all." China took a roll from the breadbasket and haphazardly spread butter on it.

"Have you changed your mind?" Jackson reached for his own roll.

"No. It's just my world has gotten really complicated.

This process is important to me, too, and I just have to figure out a way to balance it all."

Jackson reached across the table and took China's hand. "I realize we're just getting to know each other, and that I'm merely a lowly doctor compared to your role as in-house counsel to a billion-dollar company, but if there's anything I can do to help you with whatever…I'm here."

China saw the curious onlookers watching them as she slowly withdrew her hand. "I appreciate that, but we both know you're no lowly anything, Mr. Chief of Pediatric Surgery for the fourth-largest children's hospital in the country."

Jackson smirked. "Well, we both know how busy our professional lives are, but what I don't know is why you would sign up with More Than Just Dating. You have to be beating off the guys with a stick."

China's cell phone rang. "Excuse me." She fished her phone out of her purse, read the screen and sent the caller to voice mail before setting it facedown on the table. "Well, actually—"

"Two house salads with chicken," the waiter said, placing plates in front of them both. "Can I get you anything else?"

Jackson gestured with his hand for China to speak first. "No, everything looks great. Thank you," she said, reaching for her utensils.

Jackson nodded his agreement and started cutting into his salad. "You were saying…"

China held up her right index finger, as she had just placed a forkful of food into her mouth. "Dating has never been a priority. I wanted to focus on my career. I guess I got that from my mother."

"You didn't share much about your family in your profile questionnaire. I know there's more to your story than just being an only child raised by a single military mother," Jackson said, giving her a knowing look.

China groaned. "Are you sure you want to hear my sad, yet not so sad, story?"

"We're supposed to be getting to know each other, remember?" Jackson picked up his bread and took a bite.

"My parents met when they were in their twenties and stationed in Paris."

"Sounds romantic." He took a drink from his glass.

"According to my mom, it was, and very much forbidden." China took another bite of her salad.

"Why, because they were a mixed couple?"

"No, because the military has rules against fraternizing, no matter what color you are," she said, wiping her mouth with the extra napkins on the table. "They had a brief relationship before they were stationed in different parts of the world."

"So, what happened? Your mother got pregnant and had to raise you on her own?" he incorrectly guessed.

"They both followed their dreams down very different paths. My father retired after providing twenty-five years of service and went into politics, while my mother went on to become a three-star general."

"Wow, impressive parents."

China nodded. "My mother was a very impressive woman."

"Your father, too," Jackson said as if she needed to be reminded.

"I guess." China took another sip of her drink while she checked the time on her phone.

"You have someplace to be?" Jackson took a bite of his food.

"I have a press conference in about an hour." China used her fingers to pop a piece of chicken into her mouth.

"When did you come into the picture?"

"Twenty years after they first met, they ran into each other again at a military conference. And—"

"Sparks flew and nine months later you were born," he concluded.

He sure is a romantic. "Something like that, only having a kid so late in life wasn't something either of them expected. My mother was thrilled because she didn't think she'd ever have a child. My father, on the other hand, not so much."

"I'm sorry," he said, his brows furrowed. "Did you see him growing up?"

"No." China had to fight back the sense of loss from not having a father in her life that tended to sneak up on her at the worst times. "He offered financial support but didn't think contact was necessary. So it was just me and Mom. While it was hard sometimes, I loved every minute I had with her."

"What do you mean 'hard'?"

China picked up her phone, read the screen and sent Alexander's second call to voice mail. China's first instinct was to answer Alexander's call like always and accept whatever ridiculous excuse he had for interrupting her lunch and run to his side. She wanted to do that more than ever but she knew she had to move forward.

"Mom had me in her late forties, making her much older than most of my friends' parents. Between the physical aspect of her job taking a toll on her body and having to spend so much time in the harsh sun, my mother's skin wrinkled…a lot. A number of times she was mistaken for my grandmother instead of my mother." China's mind flashed back to when she was fifteen and had made all types of excuses to her mother as to why she never had friends over or went to sleepovers herself. How she just found it easier to let people think she lived with an over-protective grandmother rather than deal with her own feelings of insecurity about her mother. China brushed away a lone tear.

"Are you okay?" Concern overtook his face.

"Yes. It's been nearly eight years since she passed, and I still miss her so much." China's voice cracked.

"I understand," Jackson said.

"Enough about me, your turn." China took a final bite of her food.

"What do you want to know—more about my family or my dating life?" he asked, pushing his empty plate aside.

China glanced at her watch. "Well, since I'm going to have to leave for my press conference soon, how about you tell me a little more about your dating preferences?"

Jackson grinned. "Finding women to date has never been an issue. Finding the right one is another story."

"What's your definition of Miss Right?"

Jackson used his napkin to wipe his mouth before placing it on the table. He gifted her with a sexy smile and said, "She's a strong and very beautiful woman. Fiercely independent and knows what she wants. Not to mention she loves chicken salad and Arnold Palmers."

A slow smile spread across China's face. *I wonder what Alexander's definition of Miss Right would be, if he even wanted one. Stop it! If you want this to work, you've got to move past these feelings for Alexander.* "How about dinner tonight at my place?" she invited a grinning Jackson.

Alexander sat at his desk, reading over his statement for the press conference, but he was finding it hard to concentrate. He picked up his phone and called China's number, only to be sent to voice mail a second time. "Dammit!"

"What's wrong?" Brice asked, walking into Alexander's office. "Or should I say, what *else* is wrong?"

"Nothing. Have you found the so-called pile of money I'm supposed to have saved and funneled off somewhere?" His anger was unmasked.

"Of course not," Brice said, his eyebrows coming together. "A, you get that we *all* know you had nothing to do with any of this, right?"

"Have you figured out how we can prove that?" he snapped back.

"Not yet," Brice said, crossing his arms.

"Then what the hell are you doing in here?" he asked. "Get back to work."

Brice got up, walked to the door and closed it. He turned and faced his brother. "What the hell is wrong with you, and who do you think you're talking to?"

Alexander stood and came from around his desk to stand toe-to-toe with Brice. "I'm talking to you…*little* brother." His voice had a sharp edge to it.

"I'm not too little to kick your butt," Brice said with a raised chin.

The two men stood staring each other down for several seconds. Alexander pushed out a breath and dropped his shoulders. He ran his right hand through his hair. "Sorry, man." Alexander returned to his desk and sat down.

"What's going on with you? This can't just be about the EPA coming after us." Brice took a seat in a chair across from his brother's desk.

Alexander gave his head a slow shake. "No. It has nothing to do with the EPA."

"Then what? Talk to me before you lose it in front of someone you shouldn't, like our mother."

Alexander met his brother's gaze. "I slept with China on Friday night and she's acting like it didn't happen. Like it meant nothing and nothing has changed. She says she doesn't want it to ruin our friendship."

"Wait, you slept with China...China Edwards, your best friend?" Brice asked, scratching the side of his head.

"Yes! How many Chinas do you know, man?" Alexander questioned, looking at his brother like he'd never seen him before.

"Okay, just confirming what I heard was correct. Wow, you finally hit that."

Alexander's lips drew back in a snarl and he rose so fast he sent his chair flying backward. "Don't you dare talk about her like that," he said through gritted teeth, pointing his right index finger at his brother.

Brice held up both hands in surrender. "Chill, man, damn. I was just trying to see how real this was."

Alexander took a deep breath and released it slowly. He picked up his chair and sat back down. "Sorry."

"You have got to pull it together."

"Yeah I do. It's just..." Alexander turned and stared out the window.

"It's just sleeping with China has you all messed up. You didn't realize how deep your feelings went and now she is acting as if it didn't even matter...that you don't matter."

Alexander turned to face his brother. "Damn, man, you sound like you were there."

Brice dropped his head for several moments before he lifted it to meet his brother's inquisitive gaze. "I have been there. Hell, I'm still there...remember."

"Sorry, man. I keep forgetting." Alexander could see the pain in his brother's eyes.

"Wish I could. Enough about my failed marriage and pending divorce, that's another story. The question is, what do you want? No disrespect, A, but China's not really your type."

Alexander's brows knitted together. "What do you mean?"

"Her beauty isn't in question, and when it comes to business, she's you but in a nicer suit. Now, while your women are notably striking and smart, they're also temporary. We all know China's looking for more. She doesn't want to be another conquest."

"But she's not."

"How does she know that? Remember who we're talking about. China knows you—hell, she knows all of us as well as we know each other," Brice reminded his brother, shaking his head; China was family to them all.

Alexander nodded. "True. So what do I do?"

"What do you want…really?"

"I don't know yet. I guess I wanted a chance to figure that out," Alexander admitted.

"Well, she's told you what she wants." Brice shrugged. "Give it to her."

"What?" Alexander frowned.

"Keep being her best friend—"

"But—"

"Let me finish." Brice sat forward in his chair. "What's the best part of your relationship?"

Several big and small moments he'd spent with China flashed through his mind and he couldn't help but smile. Alexander sighed. "She gets me. We just have fun together."

"Then keep doing that. Show her that the sex hasn't changed anything," he offered.

"But it has."

Brice nodded. "And it has for her, too. Just make it easy for her to admit it to herself."

"What if that doesn't work?" Alexander's heart started racing, and his hands fisted on the desk.

"You'll still have your friend. More importantly, you have *got* to keep that possessive behavior thing you got going on right now under control."

"You're right. Thanks, man."

"Anytime." Brice walked to the door. "Besides, I wasn't looking forward to explaining to our mother why I had to beat you down in your own office."

Alexander reared back in his chair, clapped his hands and laughed. "Now you got jokes."

After his brother left, Alexander turned in his chair and stared at the photo of himself and China. "This isn't over... far from it." Alexander's cell phone rang and he viewed the screen, thinking it had to be China finally calling him back, only to be disappointed. He sent the caller to voice mail. The beautiful face that appeared on his phone was an unwanted interruption.

He stood and headed for the door.

Chapter 5

Alexander walked into the windowless executive conference room to find China standing across the room, next to his mother and cousin Kristen; they appeared to be deep in conversation. The blue suit and stiletto heels China wore showcased her body perfectly, and Alexander was having a hard time keeping his eyes away from parts of her body that *his* body desperately wanted to revisit.

Alexander started to make his way over to China, but stopped when he felt a slap on his back. "Nice job at the press conference, big bro," Brice said, entering the conference room.

"Great job, A," Morgan seconded, following Brice.

"Thanks," Alexander replied with a nod.

"Oh, good, everyone's here." Victoria walked up to her children with her arms extended and offered her cheek for a more appropriate greeting. All three hugged and kissed their mother before taking seats at the six-seat oval mahogany table with red-leather wingback chairs around it. China stood in the corner of the room, next to a full glass bar, holding a tablet at her chest.

Victoria reached for one of the bottles of water that had been placed in the center of the table. She cracked the seal, sat in the chair at the head of the table and said, "Before China brings us up to speed on the EPA's claim and our response, I'd like to take a moment to salute the excellent job everyone did at the press conference." Victoria's eyes scanned the room. "I know we're in for a difficult few months, but I think getting out in front of these ridiculous accusations and proclaiming our innocence, promising to get to the bottom of these unsubstantiated charges, was the only way to control the story. Now, China, please tell us where we are on our response to the EPA."

"Yes, Victoria." China moved closer to the table, where she and Alexander reached at the same time for a controller that sat at the end of the table. His hand grazed the top of hers and their eyes met. China quickly pulled her hand back. "Sorry," she said, breaking eye contact.

"No problem." Alexander picked up the remote and handed it to her.

"Thanks…"

China hit a button and a large, wall-mounted mirror transformed into a television screen. She sat her tablet upright on the table and ran her hands over the keys. The dancing cats that had been jumping around the screen of the tablet suddenly appeared on the television screen and laughter broke out in the room.

"You choose dancing cats as your screensaver? I thought you didn't like cats," Brice said.

"She loves them—she's just allergic to most of them," Alexander explained, giving China a small wink.

"Enough. China…" Victoria rolled her hand, instructing China to proceed. It was like she was a queen waving to her subjects.

"Sorry about that." China hit a couple more keys and a presentation appeared on the screen. "Let's go through the filing." China picked up a laser pointer. "I'd like to highlight a few things for everyone."

Alexander sat back in his chair and watched China brief the family on her current findings, the initial game plan and a strict time schedule for when the official responses to the EPA claims were due, important information that he couldn't seem to concentrate on. All he could think about was the slight sway of her hips as she walked around the room, gesturing toward the screen. The cute way her brow furrowed when she explained key details that she found troubling or confusing and the sexy way her lips curved up when she laughed. Alexander had always loved China's laugh. He thought about the first time he'd heard it.

Alexander stood in line at his favorite soul-food restaurant down the street from his law school. He was reading through his emails when he heard hysterical laughter that ended with a snort. He looked around to find that it was coming from a pretty young woman without a bit of makeup on her face, wearing a white Harvard Law T-shirt, jean shorts and tennis shoes, and with her hair pulled up in a high, messy ponytail. She was holding two large books from the law library. Alexander recognized the big red sticker that ran across their spines.

"Those aren't supposed to be removed from the library," he said, smiling down at the gorgeous woman.

"Excuse me?" China stopped in her tracks, placing her free hand on her hip.

"Those books." He pointed with his index finger. "They aren't supposed to be checked out of the law library. So

either you stole them, or someone made an exception for you."

"I don't see how either is your business," she snapped back.

"Spunky, I like that." Alexander smirked.

China rolled her eyes. *"Good for you,"* she said, turning her back on him.

"I guess I'll just have to report you...China Edwards," he said, having read the student ID clipped to her belt.

China quickly turned back to face him. *"If you must know, they made an exception for me."*

"I get that. People make exceptions for me all the time," he said, laughing.

"I won't," she declared confidently.

"No, and you still haven't," he murmured, breaking away from the past.

"What was that, son?" Victoria asked.

"Excuse me?" he replied, sitting up straighter in his chair.

Alexander's brothers laughed until Victoria rose slowly from her seat, her face expressionless. She walked around the table to where her firstborn sat. "Are we boring you, son? Is your mind elsewhere, perhaps?" she asked, tilting her head slightly to the side.

Alexander sighed. "Of course not, Mother," he replied, annoyed—not at the idea of being caught daydreaming, but at the thought that he couldn't multitask, a fact China certainly knew firsthand. Alexander's eyes cut to China and the corner of her mouth rose. It was as if she could read his mind.

China came and stood next to Victoria. "Everyone has their assignments, Victoria, and as long as we all stay focused—" she patted Victoria on the shoulder "—we'll be fine."

Alexander knew China was correct. Right now the business would be everyone's priority. He would lead the day-to-day operations of their organization, while China continued to ensure that they were doing so ethically and legally.

"I'm sure we will, my dear. Now, I have an appointment to get to. I'll leave you to your respective jobs." Victoria gathered her things and headed for the door.

"I'll walk out with you," China said, picking up her tablet. "I have a great deal to do myself."

"Well, that was a total waste of time," Morgan proclaimed, getting to his feet.

"What are you talking about?" Brice questioned Morgan with a deep frown on his face.

"We're no closer to finding the bastard that got all this mess started."

"It's only been a couple of days. We still have a lot to do," Brice reminded his brother.

"Yeah, and Mother needs to let us do it. All these update meetings that Mom likes make me crazy," Morgan said.

"I agree," Alexander supported his brother.

Brice's brows drew together. "Why are you two acting like this is a new thing for her? Do you remember how she was when we were kids?"

"Yeah, we couldn't play Uno without her making sure we understood the rules of the game," Alexander reminded them, the corner of his mouth turning up.

"By the time we were done discussing all the rules, I didn't want to play anymore," Morgan confessed.

The three brothers laughed.

"I'm heading out to the rigs. Call me if you need me."

Morgan walked out of the room after giving both his brothers the peace sign.

"So…" Brice said, nodding his head.

Alexander's phone beeped. He removed it from his pocket and read the screen. "So…what?" he asked, not looking up from his phone.

"I see you've done absolutely nothing about China since we last spoke."

Alexander checked his watch. "You mean within the last few hours…no," he said sarcastically.

"Well, you're right about one thing. China is definitely acting like things are business as usual between you two."

"I know, but I have a plan." Alexander smirked.

Brice clapped his left hand on the table and laughed. "This I have to hear."

Alexander's phone beeped again and he read the message. "Sorry, little brother, I got to go. Duty calls," he said, walking out of the conference room. *You may not know it yet, but, China, you're number one on my to-do list. I might not know what comes next, but I'm certainly willing to find out.*

China walked past her assistant's empty desk and into her office, where she placed her tablet on her glass-topped wooden desk before flopping down into her large white-leather wingback chair. She had barely kept it together when Alexander's hand grazed hers. China couldn't understand how such a benign act could have such an effect on her; she'd had difficulty breathing, her heart flipped and her head started spinning. She was just thankful she got through her presentation without making a complete fool of herself.

China had been trying to convince herself that her night with Alexander hadn't affected her beyond the physical, that their relationship was still on solid footing. Too bad her heart and body didn't get that memo. "Okay, China, you're being ridiculous, running away from Alexander like that. You work together and he's your best friend. He may not be the best person to have a romantic relationship with, or share a child with, for that matter, but he is the closest thing you have to family. You have got to pull it together," she said out loud.

"China, you talking to yourself again?" her good friend Porsche asked, as she entered China's office holding two large cups. The tall, dark-skinned beauty was a successful, high-end real estate agent and became friends with China after she'd sold her her first property several years earlier. She took the seat in front of China's desk and handed her the drink. "Strawberry lemonade, extra sweet, just the way you like it."

"No, that's just how *you* like it, but thanks," China said, taking a sip. "What are you doing here, Porsche, and how did you get past Joyce?"

"Joyce wasn't at her desk and I was in the area showing a property. I thought I'd bring you an afternoon pick-me-up," she explained.

China gave Porsche a sideways glance. "Really? And this little visit has nothing to do with my lunch date with Jackson?"

"Of course not." Porsche took a sip of her drink. "Now if you *want* to tell me about it…"

"There's nothing to tell." China turned to face her computer.

"There you go, doing that evading thing you do again." Porsche wrapped her lips around the straw and took a big pull.

China turned back to face her friend. "What evading thing?"

Porsche shrugged. "Oh, I don't know—the fact that you change the subject whenever you don't want to deal with something."

"Like what?"

"Like the fact that you slept with possibly the most arrogant man in the world and you're probably regretting it," she stated confidently.

"The only thing I regret is telling you about it." China got up and quickly went to close the door.

Porsche rolled her eyes skyward. "Then what's wrong?" She dug through her bag and pulled out her buzzing phone. She checked her messages before placing it on the desk.

"What makes you think anything is wrong?" China asked, returning to her seat.

"Maybe the fact that you called me Sunday, upset and feeling guilty about having to cancel on Jackson."

"That was work related."

"We both know you were relieved that you had to cancel on Jackson. You were still reeling over having had hot, nasty sex with your so-called best friend." Porsche's face contorted as though she had just smelled something unpleasant.

China placed her elbows on her desk, dropped her face into both palms and shook her head. "I still can't believe I did it," she said, her voice barely audible.

"Me, either. So, what, he's acting funny with you now?" She took another drink from her cup. "You need to be more like Rihanna and become a savage and say 'To hell with him.'"

China dropped her hands and met her friend's eyes. "Not at all. It's me. Every time he gets near me, I start to feel…funny."

"Oh…" Porsche gave China the side eye. "You mean horny."

"Yeah." China gave her head a small shake. "I have to get it together. I have plans that don't include Alexander," she proclaimed as her door opened.

"Someone call my name?"

Chapter 6

Porsche stood and folded her arms across her chest. "You must've misunderstood while you were clearly ear hustling."

Alexander mimicked Porsche's stance and smiled. "It's always good to see you, too, Porsche...and I wasn't eavesdropping," he said matter-of-factly. Alexander was fighting the desire to kiss that worried look off China's face.

China's eyes widened when Porsche dropped her hands to her hips. She rose and quickly came around her desk to stand next to her volatile friend. "What can I do for you, Alexander?" she asked.

"I thought we could talk."

"You thought wrong." Porsche's eyebrows came to attention. "You're on my time, and we both know how you feel about doing things in a timely manner."

Not this again. I really thought we'd gotten past this.

Porsche was still angry at Alexander for pulling out of

a real estate project because she couldn't move the deal forward within his required time frame. A time frame Porsche thought was arbitrary and ridiculous; the loss had caused her to miss a self-imposed goal.

Alexander placed his right hand over his heart. "I apologize for my rude interruption," he said, offering both women a wide smile.

"Not accepted." Porsche returned to her chair, picked up her phone and started going through her messages.

"Ignore Captain Petty over there. Did you need something in particular?"

"Yes, I'd like to have dinner with my friend tonight, if you're available?"

"As a matter of fact she's not," Porsche volunteered with a half grin. "She has plans already." Porsche turned her attention back to her phone.

"Come on, Porsche, this is important. I'm sure you wouldn't mind rescheduling. I'd owe you one." As much as Alexander hated to give her the upper hand, it was a sacrifice he was willing to make in order to spend an evening alone with China.

"Actually—" Porsche looked up, smiling "—I'm not her date tonight," she advised him proudly, crossing her arms and legs. "I'm pretty sure the gorgeous hunk she *is* seeing tonight won't be giving up his time with her, either."

"Porsche, please…" China said.

"Date? You have another date?" Alexander asked, unable to hide the surprise in his voice but trying to keep his anger in check.

"Yes, and why are you looking at me like that? I do date, remember." China crossed her arms across her chest, a move that had Alexander's body responding in a way he wished it wouldn't in that moment.

Keep it in check, man. The last thing you need to do is

push China further away. "How could I forget?" He placed his hands in his pockets.

"Seems to me like you keep trying," Porsche chimed in.

Alexander frowned and glared at Porsche. "Can you give us—"

"Nope. My time, remember?"

"I really wish you two would stop acting like a couple of rival teenagers," China declared.

"She started it," Alexander said, knowing how ridiculous he sounded.

"Did not," Porsche defended herself.

They stared at each other in silence. China returned to her desk and took a seat. She placed her hands on her desk, one over the other. "Alexander, we both have a lot of work to do and I should get back to it. As for dinner, I have to take a rain check."

"Fine. Goodbye, Porsche," Alexander said before turning to leave.

"Boy bye," she said.

China took a deep breath before releasing it slowly. She turned her attention to her friend. "Do you have to do that?" She frowned.

"Do what?" Porsche asked, offering her a sheepish look.

"Push his buttons like that. And since when did you start using colloquialisms?" Her frown deepened.

"Since now. Besides, he deserves my contempt," she insisted.

"Why? Because of one blown business opportunity? One that would have made you peanuts compared to the ones you've made before and since, several of which were referrals Alexander made to you."

"Your point?" Porsche sat with her arms crossed like a defiant child.

"My point is…get over it."

Porsche sighed and dropped her arms. "I just hate that he wouldn't admit that his timeline was ridiculous and inflexible. He has yet to apologize for the fact that I missed my goals."

China sat back in her chair and shook her head. "First off, his timeline for that deal was tight, which was not ridiculous, and it certainly wasn't flexible. There were a number of things built around it so it couldn't have been changed."

"He could have—"

"Let me finish." China held up her hand. "Second, your so-called *missed sales goals—*" she emphasized with air quotes "—were not a real miss and we both know it. Finally, all those referrals he sent you after that deal—I believe there were five—*was* his way of apologizing." China tilted her head and raised her left eyebrow before turning to face her computer.

Porsche stood and collected her things. "I guess you might have a small point there. I should let you get back to work."

"I'll call you later." China continued to run her fingers across her computer keys.

"Okay." Porsche stood at China's door. "What's the name of that expensive-ass whiskey you two drink?"

"Black Label, why?" she asked, a slow smile crawling across her face.

Porsche shifted her weight from one leg to the other. "I thought I might send Alexander a bottle. You know, just as a thank-you for the referrals."

China smirked. "Of course."

Feeling angry, jealous and somewhat out of control, Alexander returned to his office. He walked through the lounge over to his bar and poured himself a drink. The golden liquid had no time to rest in the crystal glass. Alexander tossed it back so fast he barely felt the taste of the whiskey on his tongue. He gripped the empty glass so tight that it shattered in his hand. Alexander wasn't sure if it was the breaking of the glass or the sight of his own blood that surprised him more.

"Dammit!" He dropped what was left of his glass in the trash and quickly retrieved the pieces that had dropped to the floor and discarded them, as well. He went over to his bathroom to nurse his injury. After bandaging his hand, Alexander returned to his bar and poured himself another drink.

"Well, I guess it's close enough to five o'clock," a voice called from behind him. "Pour me one, too." Brice stood next to Alexander's desk holding a couple of file folders, his body angled toward the lounge.

Alexander dropped his shoulders and didn't bother to look up from his pouring. "Neat?"

"It's whiskey," Brice said, as though that was the most ridiculous question he'd ever heard.

Alexander walked over to his desk, handed his brother a glass and took his seat. "Are those the tax summaries?" He pointed to the folders that now sat on the edge of his desk with his glass.

"Yeah. What happened to your hand?" Brice took a drink from his glass and sat down in front of his brother's desk.

"Nothing. How do we look?" he forced himself to ask. Alexander knew he had to focus on work; otherwise he'd be back in China's office, demanding that she tell him about her date. This behavior was completely out of character but seemed to be his norm lately. Alexander knew if he wanted to make a clear and rational decision about how to move his relationship with China forward, he had to get off the emotional rollercoaster he was on.

"That hand doesn't look like nothing to me and we're good as always."

"Did the last of the expenses for the Smerconish land deal get entered in time to be included in the summary?" Alexander's jaw tightened.

"Are you seriously asking me that question…about *my* job?" Brice's eyes bored into his brother. "Of course, and all I need is for you and Mom to sign off on the summaries. As soon as you do, we'll start the electronic submission process. Our first-quarter taxes will be submitted with time to spare."

"Good, all we need is to have the IRS breathing down our necks, too."

"Now stop deflecting. What caused that nothing?" Brice asked, pointing to his brother's hand.

Alexander tossed back the last of his drink. "China's dating someone."

"And?" Brice swallowed his own drink.

"And it might be something." Alexander rubbed his temples with the palms of his hands.

"How do you know it's something? Sometimes a date is just a date."

"I said she's *dating* someone." Alexander rose and looked out his office window. The thought made his chest hurt. "Someone she hasn't even talked to me about."

"China's dated before. What is it about this guy that's making you so crazy?"

Alexander stood silently as images of China wearing a wedding dress, walking down an aisle toward another man and being rolled out of the hospital in a wheelchair holding a baby invoked pain unlike anything he'd ever experienced. These thoughts and emotions had Alexander leaning forward, gripping his credenza.

Brice stood. "Are you all right?"

Alexander could hear the concern in his brother's voice. He took a deep breath and exhaled slowly before turning to face him. "I'm fine."

Brice folded his arms across his chest. "You're about as far from fine as you can get. Go talk to her, man. Let her know how you feel."

"That's just it. I don't know how I feel." Alexander gripped the back of his chair.

"I think you do, and I think it scares the hell out of you. I know I'm the last person who should be giving advice about any of this, but I think you should fight for China. That is, if you really want her. And I do mean *her* and everything that that means. Including giving China the children she wants and in the time frame she wants them."

Alexander pulled his chair back and sat down. He reached across his desk and picked up the folder. "I'll go over these with Mom tonight. I have to go drop some other stuff off that she forgot to take home."

Brice held up his hands, turned and headed for the door.

"Brice…"

"Yeah," he said, looking over his shoulder, his right hand resting on the doorknob.

"Thanks."

"Anytime, A."

China yawned and checked her watch. "Time to go." She'd started gathering up her things when her office phone rang. China stared at the phone a moment, waiting for her assistant to pick it up, then she remembered that Joyce had had to leave early. China hit the speaker button and said, "China Edwards."

"Hello, Ms. Edwards, this is Ida Brown, your personal relationship coach from More Than Just Dating."

China picked up the phone's receiver. "Good afternoon, Mrs. Brown. Nice to hear from you again. What can I do for you?"

"I just want to follow up to see how things were developing with you and Jackson Weatherly," she said.

That's a good question. They were going great until I made love with Alexander. "Things are going well, thank you for asking."

"That's great to hear. As you know, we here at More Than Just Dating want you to be satisfied with your decision to become a part of our family as well as with the ultimate choice you make."

I might have been very satisfied with my decision if I hadn't opened Pandora's box. You've got to get these feelings for Alexander under control. "Yes, everyone there has been wonderful," China complimented her.

"We have received several additional requests from men to meet you. They have all met your very specific criteria. How would you like for us to handle these requests?"

China had to hold back her laughter as she recalled the number of intense meetings, phone calls and special requests the management team of More Than Just Dating had to endure prior to her final decision to move forward with their agency. "For now, please change my account status to yellow." *The last thing I need is to add more fuel to this already raging fire.*

More Than Just Dating has three ways to identify their clients' current search status; green identified clients as seeking a match, yellow as a match possibly found and red as a match found. "That's wonderful news. I thought you and Mr. Weatherly would make a good match."

Initially China thought she and Jackson were a good

match. However, now that her feelings had been compromised, she didn't know exactly what that change meant and how it would affect any potential relationship with Jackson.

"It's early," China admitted.

"Do you see yourself moving forward in a relationship with Mr. Weatherly, or is he more suitable as a donor?"

China's eyes lasered in on a small framed photo of herself and Alexander from their law school graduation. The photo sat on a small antique table placed to the right of her desk, and her heart turned over. "I'm not sure which direction I'll end up taking."

"Well, either way, Mr. Weatherly is a great choice. Oh, my, it's after six. I won't keep you any longer. Have a good evening."

"Thank you," China said before ending the call. She stood, picked up her purse and stared at another picture of herself and Alexander. She walked over to it and ran her fingers across the picture in its frame. "No, China, you have no idea what direction you're going to take."

Chapter 7

After stopping by his place to change into something more casual—jeans, a dark blue button-down shirt and leather shoes—Alexander made his way to his mother's house. He stood at the front door, holding two boxes of files and used his left elbow to ring the doorbell.

"Good evening, Alexander. Let me help you with that," offered Gregory, Victoria's longtime devoted butler, reaching for the top box.

"No, thanks, Gregory, I got it. Mom's expecting me," Alexander explained.

The butler led Alexander through the entrance hall into a grand foyer where Italian marble ran. To the left of the hall was a formal living room, extravagantly decorated, which spoke to Victoria's over-the-top style. The formal dining area, to its right, opened onto a large executive kitchen, and had a more eclectic feel. The two men walked past a two-sided marble staircase into a large family room adorned with dark blue and white contemporary furnishings.

"Why don't you put the boxes here for now?"

Alexander dropped his box and said, "Thanks. Where's my mother?"

"She's upstairs in the theater. Can I get you anything to drink or eat?"

"No, thank you." Alexander reached into one of the boxes he'd held and pulled out two file folders. "I just need to speak with her for a minute."

"You know the way," Gregory said before exiting through a side door that led into a casual dining area and the kitchen.

Alexander made his way back to the foyer and up the wide marble staircase, taking the stairs two at a time. To his right, at the end of the hall, was a set of closed double doors. Alexander knocked and a small voice beckoned him to enter. He opened the door and walked into a room where only the light from a seventy-inch TV pierced the darkness.

Alexander closed the door behind him and called out, "Mother…?"

"Yes, darling. Hit the dimmer switch and come join me," Victoria instructed.

Alexander felt for the switch on the wall and turned the knob until the room filled with light. Victoria was sitting in one of the ten large, dark-leather reclining chairs that faced the screen. Using her left hand, she waved her son forward.

"Good evening, Mother," Alexander said, leaning forward and kissing her on the cheek. "I brought the boxes you requested. They're in the family room."

"Thank you, son. I'll have Gregory bring them up to my office later."

"I also—"

"Have a seat, Alexander." Victoria reached for the remote and hit the mute button. "I just started a movie but I can restart it. Care to join me?"

"No, thanks, I'm good." Alexander waved off her offers with both hands.

Victoria took a drink from her stemless wineglass. "Plans tonight...anyone I know?" she asked, smiling.

"No, Mother, I have no plans. I brought you the boxes like you asked, along with the first-quarter tax summaries you need to review and sign. Brice would like to start the filing process tomorrow. I thought we could go over them tonight."

Victoria sighed and took another sip from her glass. "Sometimes I wish you weren't so much like me. All business and no fun isn't good, darling." She held up her hand, stopping his protest before he could even open his mouth. "I mean fun with someone of substance. Someone you can build a future with."

"Look who's talking," he countered. "Dad's been gone for how many years now?"

"Oh, I have fun... I even date," she said, offering a wicked smile.

Alexander shuddered and wanted to kick himself for even taking the bait.

"The difference is, son, you and your brothers are my future, so I'm set. I'll really be good when one of you decides to give me grandbabies." Victoria's left eyebrow rose.

Alexander rolled his eyes and plopped down in a chair next to Victoria. "Here we go..."

"It's your life. Give me the damn files," Victoria ordered, offering her left palm.

Alexander pressed his lips together and complied. He knew whenever his mother became annoyed or even angry there was no talking to her in that moment. Alexander handed her the file and sat back quietly as she reviewed the documents in silence.

After several minutes, Victoria looked up from the file and asked, "Are all the Smerconish expenses included in this file?"

"Yes, ma'am," he replied. Alexander had learned a long time ago that the only thing that could be predicted about Victoria Kingsley was her methodical approach and detailed questions when it came to the business.

Victoria reached into a pouch connected to her chair and pulled out a pen. She signed in all the appropriate places before handing the file back to her son. "I'd like for you to run that past China before Brice starts submitting it to the IRS."

"China…why?" Alexander sat up in his chair.

Victoria turned her body slightly in her chair to face her son. "Let's see, China is our chief counsel and has a brilliant mind for business. She has a photographic memory filled with years of our tax data and, oh, yeah, because I said so."

"Fine, I'll have her look over it first thing in the morning," he reluctantly agreed, not thinking this added scrutiny was necessary.

"No, tonight. It's still early and I'm sure she's up." One corner of her mouth rose.

What's she up to? "How can you be so sure?" Alexander asked, grimacing.

"I saw her before she left this afternoon. She was talking about the dinner she was making for her date." Victoria took a whiff of her wine before taking another sip.

Alexander felt as though he'd been slapped but he refused to let his mother see his annoyance. "Well, I certainly shouldn't interrupt her evening." Although he remembered what happened the last time he'd interrupted her date and had to fight back his smile.

"This is business and China knows how important these tax reports are. I'm sure she'll be fine with a small interruption." Victoria pulled a blanket over her legs. "Besides, she reads as fast as a hiccup. I'm sure the visit will be brief. Since when did you let anything or anyone stand in the way of what you want?"

Good question.

Victoria reclined in her chair, hit the remote control and restarted her movie. "Turn off the lights on your way out. Goodnight, son."

Alexander shook his head at the dismissal. "Goodnight, Mother."

China walked into her clean, gray-and-white kitchen with the red stainless-steel appliances that hadn't been used for quite some time, and by the look of things, it didn't appear that would be changing anytime soon. She stood barefoot at her granite-topped island wearing a black lace tank top and shorts set, her hair wrapped in a towel and her face free of makeup. China reached for the bottle of Stella Rosa red that she had opened earlier and topped off her glass.

"Nice lingerie and a good bottle of wine for another night alone? You were right to cancel your date," she said out loud as she poured. China sat on a stool at the island, tapping her fingernails against the wine bottle. "You can't have dinner with one man while constantly thinking about another, China." She took a drink from her glass and held it at her chin. "It was just sex…great sex, but still sex." She nodded. "Who are you kidding? That was a welding of our mind, body and soul."

After sitting in silence for several minutes, China slid

off the stool, picked up her glass and returned the wine bottle to the refrigerator. She reached for the remote that lay on the glass coffee table and began channel surfing, only to quickly abandon the idea. "Too bad I read so damn fast." China sighed. "Enough talking to yourself."

She rose from her chair and turned off the television and the lights, and had just begun climbing the stairs when she heard her security system being disarmed. She stopped and stared at the door. Her heart raced, but not from fear. Only two people had her security code and a spare key: her assistant, Joyce, and Alexander. Joyce would never show up at her place unannounced, even in an emergency situation. No, only one person was arrogant enough to do such a thing, and she was actually happy about the prospect of seeing him, regardless of the reason. The door slowly opened and Alexander walked through.

China and Alexander's eyes collided. He opened his mouth to speak, but quickly closed it as his eyes roamed China's body. He turned his head, obviously taking in his surroundings. China could see the collision of fury and desire in his eyes, surely sending him into a barely contained rage, as though a realization had just hit him in the gut. Alexander's forehead creased, his nostrils flared and his chest rose and fell rapidly. His left hand fisted at his side, while his right gripped the doorknob as if it was a lifeline. Alexander reminded China of a bull that was getting ready to charge after the red flag.

"Alex, I'm alone," China said, holding his gaze. "No one's here. I'm alone." She knew she should be angry about his obvious assumption and intrusion, but his jealousy and mounting rage excited her, instead.

Alexander released a slow, labored breath, his shoulders dropped and his hands slowly relaxed. He closed and locked the door behind him but remained still. "You always dress like that when you're sleeping alone?"

"You always let yourself into other people's houses with an emergency key when it's not an emergency?" China brought her glass to her mouth and took a sip, eyeing him over the rim, trying to keep her raging hormones under control.

Alexander smirked. "This is an emergency," he said.

"How so?" China's nipples were hard as marbles, a fact she couldn't hide in her tank top.

Alexander's eyes zeroed in on China's breasts. He walked to the steps and leaned against the wall. "You didn't answer my question. You always dress like that when you're sleeping alone?" he asked, his voice low and husky.

"Yes."

Alexander pushed off the wall and climbed the stairs, stopping one step away from China. He ran the back of his hand across the front of her stomach. "Nice. Does it come in other colors?" China shivered and took a step back. A slow, sexy smile crawled across Alexander's face before he took a step forward. "What other colors do you have, China?"

"Wh-white," she whispered. China cleared her throat. "What do you want, Alex?"

Alexander removed the glass from China's hand and finished off the contents. He sat it on the step, pulled the towel from China's head, allowing her damp hair to hang free. He dropped the towel, cupped China's face with both hands and kissed her passionately on the lips. He allowed their lungs to breathe and said, "You know damn well what I want." He picked her up, and China wrapped her legs around his waist. Alexander kissed China's neck, shoulder and collarbone as he carried her into the bedroom.

China felt a pull toward Alexander, and it was unlike

anything she'd ever felt before. In that moment, she didn't care about the consequences of their actions or how it would affect their friendship. She wanted him. She pulled her top over her head, letting it fall to the floor, and guided Alexander's mouth to her breasts.

"Oh, yes…" she cried as Alexander laid her down on the bed without releasing her nipple from his possessive grip. China could feel the pressure between her legs building. "Please, Alex…please."

Alexander stood over China and toed off his shoes. He took off his shirt, and removed his pants and underwear in one swoop.

"My, my," she said, responding to his erection. China sprang forward, captured his sex with her hand and started massaging its tip. His head dropped back and he released a growl that made her smile before taking him into her mouth. She never knew pleasuring a man could bring her so much personal pleasure. Hearing Alexander's increasing sounds of satisfaction only spurred her to increase her lips' pressure.

He pushed China's shoulders and took a step back, freeing himself, "Damn, woman…"

China lay back on the bed and laughed. Alexander reached for his pants and removed a condom. "Need help putting that on?" She offered up a coy smile.

"I got it." Alexander rolled on the fine layer of protection, removed China's shorts and separated her legs with his left knee.

Alexander stood between her thighs, stroking himself with his thumb and index finger as he stared down at China. She, in turn, used the tips of her fingers to explore her body. She loved the smoldering look in Alexander's eyes, the way the pupils dilated as her hand made its way to her sex. China inserted first one, then two fingers, matching Alexander stroke for stroke. As China's breath increased and her body began to rise from the bed, Alexander dropped to his knees, pushed her hands out of the way and brought her to completion with his tongue.

"Oh, wow... I need you now," China all but begged.

Alexander kissed his way up her body, capturing her lips in a heart-piercing, sensual kiss. "I can't even explain how much I need you," he whispered.

"Show me..."

Alexander held her gaze as he slowly entered her. China wrapped her legs around his waist and he led her body in a long, slow, erotic dance. China stared into Alexander's eyes as she tried but failed to fight back tears. "I've never felt so complete."

"Neither have I," he said, kissing away her tears. "Neither have I."

With each passionate kiss and slow purposeful thrust of Alexander's hips, he permanently branded China's heart and she knew that no matter what happened between them, things would never be the same. Their zealous lovemaking resulted in them falling into a deep sleep in each other's arms.

Chapter 8

Alexander woke with China's warm body in his arms, and he'd never been happier. They'd made love most of the night and he still wanted her. The one person he trusted above all others. The person he would start and end most days thinking about was now part of his DNA. Alexander realized this was how things were meant to be between he and China and Alexander was going to make sure things stayed that way. He knew that together they could do anything, and he was just grateful he hadn't missed his opportunity.

Hearing China release a deep, satisfied breath, Alexander kissed her exposed shoulder before slowly retrieving his arm from under her neck. He made his way to the bathroom, where he used one of several unopened toothbrushes she always kept for guests. After taking a quick shower, Alexander dressed in last night's clothes and made his way downstairs to the kitchen. *If I want China to even listen to my proposition, I'd better feed her.* He opened the refrigerator, smiled and shook his head. "Well, at least you have eggs, cheese and orange juice."

China rolled onto her back, stretched out her arms and found that she was alone. She sat up as her eyes scanned the room. Seeing no sign of Alexander, she fell back onto the bed. China grabbed his pillow and inhaled. "Damn, China, what's wrong with you? You can't keep sleeping with Alex if you're serious about moving forward with your plans to create your own family with someone else. You know he can't give you what you want, so start thinking with your head and not your heart and hormones," she chastised herself.

China smiled when she was hit with the aroma of coffee. "Hmm… Alex started the coffee before he left. Excellent." She checked the time and headed to the bathroom, her muscles screaming all the way. "Damn, girl, you have got to get back to spin class."

After brushing her teeth and taking a quick shower, China walked into the large walk-in closet adjacent to her bathroom. She selected and dressed in a pleated red short-sleeved Calvin Klein dress, pulled her hair up into a tight bun and applied a minimal amount of makeup. She slipped her feet into a pair of black Louboutin shoes, grabbed her purse and phone, and made her way down the stairs; she was more than ready for that much-needed cup of coffee.

She walked into her kitchen and found Alexander at the island dressed in last night's clothes, his shirt half buttoned and his feet bare, standing in front of two plates that held omelets and toast, and pouring orange juice into two glasses. Her treacherous body started to override her brain and responded to the gorgeous man standing in her kitchen. *Focus.* China placed her phone and purse on the island next to the newspaper.

"Alexander, what are you still doing here?" China asked, picking up the paper and reading the headline: Billionaire Playboy Threatens the Environment for Money. She shook her head and immediately put it back down. "At least they spelled the names right. Thanks for bringing in the paper."

"No problem, and I was making breakfast for us. Why are *you* dressed like you're going to work?" he asked, frowning, setting the container of juice down.

"Because it's Tuesday and I am. The question is, why aren't you home doing the same thing, especially since you and the company are splattered all over this morning's newspaper? I can only imagine what's happening on social media and how our equity partners are handling the news. However, I wouldn't be surprised if Victoria is meeting with the powers that be and has already convinced them of our innocence."

China pulled her travel mug out from the cabinet and poured coffee into it. Alexander leaned against the island and folded his arms across his chest. "It's nothing we didn't expect, and yes, my mother has already met with both investment groups. I thought we'd eat. Talk about where we go from here."

"We go to work." China picked up a fork, sliced into her food and took a bite. "This is good. You made this," she asked, pointing at the omelet with her fork, "with what I had in my refrigerator?"

"Yes, can you at least sit down?" Alexander's tone was flat.

China complied and Alexander took the seat next to her. He ate two bites of his omelet and slid his plate forward. "You done?" China asked before taking a sip of her orange juice.

"I guess I wasn't that hungry after all," he said, his tone hard.

China sighed. She picked up a napkin and wiped her mouth. She turned her body toward him. "All right, let's talk." China relaxed her hands in her lap.

"After last night I thought we'd…" Alexander held her gaze in silence.

China tilted her head slightly. "What, exactly? Nothing's changed since the first time we slept together. Well, except that we broke our promise not to do it again."

"So, last night meant nothing to you?" he asked with a pained expression.

China lowered her head, briefly trying to rein in her emotions. "That's not what I'm saying."

"Then what are you saying, China?"

She raised her head and looked into his handsome face. *Keep your emotions out of this, China. He'd appreciate an honest, businesslike response.* "I adore you and your family, you know that. It's just I'm ready to have my own family. Can you honestly say you're ready for that type of relationship…with me?"

Alexander reached for China's hand. "Look, what I can honestly say is that I believe there's something special between us. Why does everything have to come back to that one issue? Why does it even have to be an issue at all… right now, anyway?"

"You know why."

"You have plenty of time for kids. I'd like to see where this could lead."

"And what if it leads us to a place we can't come back from? You're my best friend, my only family. Do you really want to risk that for what could turn out to be a sexual infatuation? I don't."

Alexander released her hand. "That's what you think? That this is a sexual infatuation."

"That's just it, Alexander, I don't know what to think." *Tell me I'm wrong. Tell me that this is real, that you're my future.*

Alexander stood. "I get it. Maybe you're right. Maybe last night was a mistake…one that definitely won't happen again."

China's heart was breaking. "Please don't be angry."

"I'm not." He slipped his feet into his shoes. "I'm glad we talked. Everything is crystal clear." Alexander leaned down and kissed China on the cheek. He picked up his keys and phone. "I'll see you later at the office."

"At the office," China murmured, wiping tears away as she watched him walk out the door. She reached for her cell phone, dialed and waited for the call to connect. "I really need to talk. Can you meet me at our spot in thirty minutes?"

Alexander made it to his office in record time. He'd changed into a clean pair of jeans and a white T-shirt, and was sitting on the couch in the lounge, putting his cowboy boots on, when his assistant, Tammy, walked into his office.

"There you are. I need you to call for the chopper."

"Good morning to you, too, sir," she replied sarcastically.

"Morning. Call for the chopper…now. I'd like to leave as soon as possible," he ordered, pulling out a small black-leather suitcase.

"Can you tell me where you're going…without snapping my head off?" she asked, glaring through narrowed eyes.

"Sorry, Tammy, bad morning. I'm going to be working the rest of the week out at the ranch." Alexander started placing the backup clothes he kept at the office in his suitcase.

"Okay. Anything I can do?"

"Yes, reschedule any in-person meetings I may have. If something urgent needs my personal attention, I'll video chat from there."

"Will do. I'll call your pilot." Tammy turned and ran into Larry, Alexander's good friend from law school.

"Thanks, Tammy," Alexander said.

"Yeah, thanks, Tammy," Larry echoed, smiling down at Tammy, but paying more attention to her chest area than her face.

"Move," Tammy said, giving him a playful shove before stepping around him to make her exit.

Alexander closed his suitcase and walked over to his desk, where he started packing up his briefcase. "What are you doing here, Larry?"

"I heard about the EPA's investigation. I know China's got your back on this, but if you need any additional backup, just let me know."

Too bad at my back isn't where I want her. "Thanks, man, and you're right, China is all about this business. We've got this. We didn't do anything wrong, and as soon as we prove that, things will get back to normal."

"I don't doubt that, but Kristen had better make sure her PR people are on point because your reputation and your company's NASDAQ ranking is taking a big hit," Larry warned.

"No worries, she's on it, and so is my mother," Alexander assured him.

"I don't doubt that. Victoria is one tough cookie." Larry took a seat in a chair across from Alexander's desk. "Where you going?" Larry asked.

"I'm—"

"Excuse me, Alexander," Tammy called, entering the office. "The helicopter will be here in twenty minutes."

"Thanks," Alexander said, frowning at the way his friend was still staring at Tammy.

She nodded and walked out the door, closing it behind her. "Damn, she fine," Larry praised her.

"She's efficient…and engaged," Alexander explained to his obviously interested friend.

"As of when?" Larry's forehead creased.

"Last month—she's been seeing the brother of one of our other employees." Alexander sat behind his desk and fired up his computer.

"Looks like everyone is getting married." Larry slouched in his chair.

Not everyone. China's face popped into his mind. Her dismissing his feelings and proposition because he was not prepared to commit to having children right now had Alexander's emotions bouncing between hurt and anger.

"So, where are you running off to?" Larry asked.

"I'm not running off anywhere. I'm going to go work at our ranch for a few days." Alexander connected a flash drive to his computer and began transferring several files.

Larry leaned forward, resting his forearms on his thighs. "How long have we known each other?"

"Too long," Alexander said sarcastically, not bothering to look up from his computer.

"Right, which means I know when something isn't right, and you deciding to go work in North Texas at your family's ranch, on a Tuesday, means something's not right. What gives?"

Alexander pushed out a breath. He removed the drive, placed it in his pocket and turned off his computer. He sat back in his chair and turned to face his friend. "My company is being attacked by the EPA for something we didn't do and the media is crucifying me for it. I think I have a right to be a little off."

"True that…"

Alexander's desk phone rang and he hit the speaker button. "Yes, Tammy."

"Your ride is five minutes away and that movie director woman called to see if you were available for dinner. She said she's staying at her usual hotel."

"Thanks, and Tammy, please send flowers to the Hilton Americas Hotel."

"What would you like the card to say?" Tammy asked.

"Just say 'next time.'"

"Will do," Tammy replied before disconnecting.

"Well, that's my cue." Larry stood. "You know what you need?"

Alexander picked up his briefcase and went to retrieve his suitcase. "What's that?"

"Something warm to ride other than your damn horse. Maybe you should rethink the flowers and send the director an invite to join you," Larry advised, laughing, as he left the office.

"Yeah, well, right idea…wrong woman. She has other plans," Alexander murmured, walking out behind his friend.

China walked into her favorite coffeehouse down from her office and heard, "Welcome to Starbucks…" She acknowledged the eager associate with a smile. China scanned the patrons until she found her target. Porsche was sitting at a table in a corner with two large cups placed in front of her, reading from a binder. China made her way to the table and took a seat.

"Thanks for meeting me so quickly." China sat her purse in one of the empty chairs at their table.

Porsche slid a cup in China's direction. "Actually I was already here working."

"Thanks. What are you working on?" she asked, before taking a sip of her drink.

"I'm reviewing another contract proposal," Porsche explained.

"That's great. All these companies are lining up to work with you, one of the best commercial real estate contractors out there." China gifted her friend with a proud smile.

"I know, and it's wonderful, but I need to bring on some legal help. Speaking of…" she said, offering up a sheepish grin.

"Oh, no." China's brows snapped together and she shook her head and left hand.

"Come on, China." Porsche brought her hands together as if she was praying. "Just this one last time."

"That's what you said the last time," China reminded Porsche.

"Okay, but I'm not sure how helpful I can be with whatever your issue is, when I'm so worried about missing anything in this proposal." Porsche smiled and batted her eyes in an exaggerated manner.

"Blackmail, really?" China glared through narrowed eyes.

"Blackmail…negotiation. You say tomato, et cetera… et cetera." Porsche used her hands to imitate balancing a scale. She pushed the binder in China's direction. "It'll take you ten minutes and then you'll have my undivided attention."

China rolled her eyes skyward before checking her watch. She knew it wouldn't take long and she could use the distraction from her emotional morning. "Fine." China accepted the binder and the highlighter Porsche was handing her. "This really is the last time."

"Agreed." Porsche sat back and watched China with a satisfied grin.

China opened the binder and ran the tip of her index finger across the page from left to right. She continued that process until she'd touched all two hundred and twelve pages of the document, stopping only long enough to highlight areas of interest in the contract she thought her friend should verify and reconsider. After less than ten minutes China closed the binder, placed the highlighter on the table and gave Porsche a smile that erased her earlier look of satisfaction.

"What?" Porsche sat up in her chair. "Did you find something?"

China intertwined her hands and sat them on top of the binder. "My turn."

Porsche threw her head back and laughed, ignoring the curious stares of the customers who were now watching them. "Touché. What's going on?"

China's shoulders dropped and she lowered her head slightly. "I…I slipped."

"You slipped? What did…" The two women stared at each other in silence for several moments. "So, now what?"

China swallowed hard. "We agreed it was a mistake."

"Another one." Porsche folded her arms. "I don't know what you want me to say here. You know how I feel about men, especially men like Alexander, and the way they treat women. Do you need me to tell you to go for it or run like hell? I can say either."

China finished the last of her coffee, drinking it down like it was some magic potion that would provide her with the answers she needed. "I don't need either. It's done. We'll remain friends and hopefully be close without fear of crossing that line again."

Porsche dropped her arms. "I think you've made the

right decision. You may have been right about the way I handled my business relationship with Alexander. However, I'm right about this. He'll never give you the family you want. He's not the type. As soon as the novelty of sleeping with you wears off, he'll be on to the next one."

China bowed her head, covered her mouth with her left hand and closed her eyes. She was so overwhelmed by her emotions she couldn't defend Alexander against this character assassination. Alexander didn't use women in the way Porsche was describing. He knew what he wanted out of his relationships and he was always clear about that with whomever he was seeing. China had no doubt that Alexander cared about her, just not in the way she was starting to care about him; their personal lives were headed in different directions.

Porsche leaned across the table, placed her hands on top of China's and whispered, "I'm sorry. Can I do anything?"

China shook her head and used her right hand to wipe away the few tears she couldn't hold back. She took a deep breath and quickly exhaled it. "I'm fine." She picked up the binder and handed it to Porsche. "I highlighted a few areas you should double-check."

"You sure you're okay?" Porsche asked, accepting the binder.

"Absolutely. Alexander and I are both professionals and our friendship means the world to us. We just need a little time and we'll get past this. Plus, we have the EPA to deal with, and that will keep us very busy these next couple of months. Good luck with that," she said, pointing at the binder.

"Thank you." The concern in Porsche's voice and on her face was evident.

China plastered on a smile that she hoped would reassure her friend. "Thanks for the coffee and the talk. Everything's going to be wonderful. I have my work and hopefully soon the family…the child I've always wanted." China rose from her chair and picked up her things. "That'll be enough for me."

Porsche stood and hugged China. "Call me if you need me."

"I will, but as far as this chapter is concerned, I won't need to." *I pray that I won't, anyway.*

Chapter 9

China sat in her chair with her left elbow on the desk and her head resting in the palm of her hand. She was flipping through a book of legal precedents when her cell phone rang. She removed it from its charging stand, read the name that appeared on the screen.

"Good afternoon, Jackson."

"Good afternoon, beautiful. How is your Wednesday going?"

China sat up, pushed away from her desk and turned her chair so that now she faced her windows. She really enjoyed the view of the city from her forty-eighth-floor office. "Busy as usual."

"Well, I won't keep you long, I just want to confirm that we're still on for dinner tonight…my place. I'm making pasta," he sang, slightly off-key.

China had enjoyed spending the last five weeks really getting to know Jackson and developing their friendship. As expected, they had a great deal in common. What she hadn't expected was how her changed feelings toward Alexander would affect any potential relationship with Jackson. No matter how hard she tried, China couldn't get Alexander, their evolving bond and all the intimacy they'd shared out of her mind and heart. China figured that, just like always, once she made the decision to move forward with Jackson, that would be that. Unfortunately, her heart was proving to be pretty stubborn when it came to letting go.

While Alexander appeared to be accepting China's choices and had moved beyond what happened between them, her mind and body hadn't gotten the message that it was time to let go. Just the sight of Alexander, or the sound of his voice, sent her up in flames. Even the thought of another man touching her was literally making her sick.

China placed her left hand over her chest and took in a couple of quick breaths. "That sounds lovely, but—"

"I know this is an especially busy time for you, China, but you have to eat."

"That's just it, Jackson, I don't think I can. It's that time of the month, and on top of that, I think I got that stupid stomach bug that's been going around."

"Oh, no, that's a nasty one, too," he said, his voice full of concern. "You're weaker now, which brings your resistance down even further, making you more susceptible to a number of viruses."

China laughed. "Thanks for the medical diagnosis, Doctor, and here I thought babies and kids were your only specialty."

"Soon you will see I'm quite good at a lot of things." Jackson chuckled.

China's stomach flipped and not in a good way.

"Seriously, I did a few rotations in several specialties

before I decided to pursue pediatrics. You need to stay hydrated, and if the nausea continues, have your doctor call you in something for it."

"Thanks, Jackson, I'll keep that in mind."

"By the way, did I leave my watch at your place?" he asked. "I don't remember putting it back on after washing your dishes the other night."

China laughed. "Yes, your precious Bulgari Diagono watch is safe and sound on my dresser."

"Great. I'll get it next time I see you."

"No problem. I have a meeting to prepare for. Let's talk later," she promised.

"I look forward to it—feel better."

China disconnected the call and stared down at the phone for several moments. She still couldn't believe that she was having such a hard time taking that next step with Jackson. China sighed and turned her chair around, only to find Alexander standing in the middle of her office with his arms folded across his chest and holding a blue file folder. He was wearing jeans and a white shirt with their company logo, a flaming phoenix, placed on the left side of the shirt just above his heart. It was the uniform he'd started wearing over the past several weeks.

It had been weeks since China and Alexander slept together and had had any type of conversation that went beyond business. China still struggled with the fact that Alexander spent almost three of the five weeks he was gone conducting their business away from the office, working between his family's and his brother's ranch without even telling her about it beforehand. This was the second time he'd pulled a disappearing stunt on her, and she still hated it, missing him as much this time as she had then.

China's breath caught in her throat. "Alexander, you startled me. I didn't hear you come in."

"I gathered that. No one's at their desk out front. Are you okay? You don't look well," he asked, his face expressionless and his tone even.

China reached for the bottle of ginger ale that Joyce had placed on her desk earlier in the day, taking several sips, hoping to calm her stomach. She couldn't be sure if it was the illness or Alexander creating such waves in her body. "I'll be fine. You know how I get when it's that time of month. Not to mention that I think I've caught that bug that's hitting everyone so hard."

"That sucks. Maybe you should go home and get some rest," he recommended.

"Maybe you should just show me whatever you're holding in your hands." China offered him her right palm.

"Stubborn as always." Alexander dropped his arms and walked up to China's desk. "This is a whittled-down version of the list of so-called potential whistle-blowers."

China accepted the folder and read the list. "This is considerably smaller than our initial listing. You sure this is it?"

"Excluding you and the rest of my family, those five people—" he pointed at the list with his right index finger "—either handled or had direct access to the EPA's disposal guidelines and the final approved policy and procedures. Now what? It's not like we can walk up to each of these people and ask if they went to the EPA and lied about us."

"Actually, we can. We have every right to interview anyone we deem appropriate in our own investigation, as long as we don't infringe on anyone's rights and they can choose to decline an interview. It's part of the employee handbook that everyone received upon being hired," China explained.

Alexander smirked and nodded. "I have a better idea.

We can have them investigated, even put them under surveillance." Alexander leaned against China's desk.

"Surveillance?" China frowned.

"Yes. Maybe we can find out who they're working for."

"What makes you think they're working with someone?" China gave him a questioning look.

"Look at the lists. None of those people could pull this
off by themselves," he said confidently.

"I'm finding it hard to believe any one of these people
would turn on us like that," she said, rubbing her temples
with the index fingers of both hands.

Alexander leaned forward. "You sure you're okay,
China?"

China dropped her hands and met his gaze. She could
feel the warmth of his breath on her face. Alexander's all-
consuming gaze had softened; she could see his concern
and it had her heart and stomach doing backflips. Before
she could respond to his question, there was a small knock
on the door. "Come in," China called out.

Alexander straightened to his full height.

"Excuse me, China." Joyce walked into the office with
her right hand holding her stomach. "I'm sorry, Alexander. I didn't realize you were in here."

"No one was at their desk when I arrived."

"My apologies, the interns are in the research depart-
ment and I was in the ladies' room…again," Joyce explained, lowering her head.

"It's fine," Alexander and China echoed.

"What's up, Joyce?" China asked, taking another sip
of her ginger ale.

"I'm not feeling well. This bug has got me really messed
up. Do you mind if I go home?" she asked.

"Not at all, I know exactly how you feel." China could

see how green her friend looked, and she could certainly empathize with her.

"Thank you." Joyce gave them a weak smile of appreciation. "It seems to be a twenty-four to forty-eight-hour thing, so I should be able to come back to work by Friday."

"No problem, just take care of yourself," China insisted, with Alexander nodding his agreement.

Joyce exited the office.

"You should take your own advice. You don't look much better," Alexander said.

"Thank you very much, Mr. Sensitive." A small smile spread across her face.

A corner of Alexander's mouth twitched. It was the first time in weeks that they'd shared any type of exchange that brought them back to the closeness they'd once shared and it actually made China feel better…complete. She missed it; she missed him.

"About this surveillance, what do you have in mind?" she murmured.

Alexander placed his hands in his pockets. "I was thinking we could bring in Meeks Montgomery from the security firm of Blake & Montgomery to handle the investigation and the surveillance. We could have them run a detailed background check on all the employees, too, just in case we missed something."

"You know him?" China questioned, her voice weak.

"I know who his father-in-law is—he did some work for my mother several years ago before he retired, turning the business over to his eldest daughter."

"What kind of work?" she asked, her curiosity piqued.

"It had something to do with the deaths of my father and uncle. Before they died they'd been working on some big deal, and the negotiations were intense. In fact, according to my mother, my dad and uncle were prepared to walk away from the deal altogether, and that would have cost others nearly a billion dollars."

China's eyes grew wide. "What kind of deal was that?"

"It was our company's first big foreign oil contract."

"That's definitely motive for foul play."

"Hence all the security we had to endure and why we ended up being raised and homeschooled on the ranch until we went off to a private high school," he explained.

"You said it was the company's first big deal. Who completed it after your father died?"

"My mother, at the same time she was having the accident investigated. I think she thought if anyone could find out if something went wrong with the initial investigation, Blake & Montgomery could. Even back then they were considered one of the best security and investigative firms in the country."

"So, did they find anything wrong?" Her eyebrows rose.

"Nope, the plane crash was due to a mechanical problem."

China's heart hurt for Alexander. "I'm sorry."

"It's cool. I'll see how soon I can get them to schedule a meeting with everyone."

"What date do you have in mind?" China turned her chair toward her computer and calendar. "Whoa…" She was hit with a wave of nausea and became very dizzy. China gripped the arms of the chair and closed her eyes.

Alexander removed his hands from his pockets, came around China's desk and knelt at her side. "Are you okay? Maybe we should get you to a doctor."

China slowly opened her eyes and looked down into a grave set of brown-and-gold orbs gazing back at her. She cupped his face with her right hand and said, "I don't need a doctor. I'll be fine, Alex, I promise."

"In all the years I've known you, your woman issues

have never done you like this. It's made you grouchy as hell, but not this."

China gave him a playful punch in the chest. "In all the years you've known me, you've never known me to have woman issues, as you put it, at the same time as a stomach virus."

Alexander held her gaze intently for several moments before standing and reaching for China's office phone. He dialed and said, "Bring my car up to the elevator." Alexander hung up the phone and lifted China out of the chair.

"What are you doing?" she whispered, her voice frail.

"I'm getting you out of here and taking you home," Alexander explained.

China was too weak to argue, so she laid her head on his chest. "Okay. Can you please grab my phone and bag?"

Alexander collected China's things, cradled her in his arms and carried her down the hall, past several inquisitive onlookers, to a private elevator. They got on and descended in silence. The doors opened to his waiting, custom-designed Aston Martin. Alexander placed China in the front passenger seat, secured her with the seat belt and closed the door. He quickly made his way around the car and got behind the wheel. China turned her head and faced Alexander. "Thank you," she whispered.

Alexander turned his head and fixed his eyes on hers. "I'm going to take care of you no matter what. You should know that by now." China offered him a weak smile. "I'd do anything for you, China."

Alexander put the car in Drive and maneuvered his way out of the parking garage. China closed her eyes. *Oh, how I wish that were true.*

Chapter 10

After using his key to open China's front door, Alexander disarmed her alarm, returned to his car and carried her into the house. Alexander knew he was going overboard by continuing to carry China into and around her house like he was but he didn't care; he missed their closeness. "I could've walked in on my own, you know," China said.

"I know." After Alexander entered the house, closing the door behind him, he climbed the stairs and took China into her bedroom, where he gently placed her on the bed. "How do you feel?"

"A little better, actually, but I do need to take a shower."

From the moment China had cupped his face, Alexander had been fighting to keep his desire for her under control. The thought of her naked body being pelted with water wasn't helping in his effort. "A shower. Need any help?" China's eyebrows came to attention. "What I meant to ask was, can I get you anything?" Alexander's phone rang and he pulled it out of his pocket.

"Saved by the bell," she teased.

He looked at the name on the screen before sending the caller to voice mail and pocketing his phone. "Hardly."

"Look, you can go. I'll be fine," China reassured him, rising from the bed and heading into her bathroom.

Alexander watched as China disappeared behind the double doors. *Travis is right; control is highly overrated.* Alexander thought back to the advice his cousin had given him several weeks ago.

Alexander stood shirtless with sweat rolling down his chest, his arm muscles expanding with each swing of the large ax he held, splitting the log in two parts with one blow.

"Hey," Travis called as he approached his cousin.

"What's up?" Alexander replied, wiping the sweat from his brow with his left hand while holding the ax low at his right side.

"You tell me. You've been here for nearly a week and I have more wood than we could use in multiple Houston winters. Not to mention your insistence on joining us on our cattle roundup last night."

"What, you don't enjoy my company?"

"Of course I do, but I also know you. You prefer your suits and office on the fiftieth floor of the Kingsley building to my hundred acres any day. At least, you used to," Travis said.

"I still do," Alexander admitted, dropping the ax. "I just needed a break." He walked over to a water station that had been placed next to a long bench.

Travis followed his cousin and stood, watching, as Al-

exander poured himself a large cup of water. "Talk to me, man."

Alexander finished off two cups of water and looked around the busy ranch before he spoke. He sat down and said, "This could take a minute."

"I'm the boss, remember?" Travis took a seat on the bench next to Alexander. He stretched out his legs and said, "I have all the time you need."

Alexander spent nearly an hour explaining the complicated current state of his relationship with China, including the advice his brother had given. He leaned forward with his elbows resting on his knees and his hands clasped together, holding up his chin.

"Now I'm here trying to rein in all these crazy emotions before I have to go back home and work side by side with her."

Travis slapped Alexander on the shoulder with his right hand. "I understand. The last thing you need is to be seen as out of control, especially with everything that's been going on and all these eyes on you lately."

"I know, and the press is relentless, too." Alexander ran his right hand back and forth through his hair.

"But I disagree with the advice Brice gave you," Travis declared, sitting up with his arms folded.

Alexander turned his head to face his cousin. "Why is that?"

"Because we're Kingsleys and we go after what we want. We don't sit by passively and wait for women to figure out if they want us or not." Travis's tone had taken on a hard edge.

Alexander laughed as he sat back. "Wow, why so hostile?"

"I'm not hostile, just stating facts."

"You sure you don't want to get something off your chest, cousin?" Alexander grimaced at Travis's mood.

"Do you want my advice or not?"

"Shoot."

"I know I'm not your average romance-novel hero, but I think you should talk to China. Tell her what's up...how you feel, and if she's not with it, bounce," Travis stated matter-of-factly.

"Walk away." Alexander stood and moved toward the stack of wood. He stopped and picked up the ax and a large log. He placed it on the chopping stand. *"Just like that?"*

Travis followed him. *"Just like that. I don't believe in playing games, especially when you really want something. Holding back...staying in control, is highly overrated."*

"I bet you're a big hit with the ladies," Alexander said, hacking into the wood.

"I am, actually." Travis pulled out his vibrating cell phone. He smiled at the message before he tapped in his response. *"Everyone knows what's up with me, and there are no games or broken promises."*

"I appreciate the talk and the advice but if you don't mind, I think I'll work on providing you with a little more wood." Alexander placed another piece of wood on the stand and raised the ax.

The sound of China's shower being turned on broke Alexander away from the past, only to have images from the night they'd shared a similar shower flood his mind. The way their greedy, soap-covered hands had run across each other's bodies, the passionate kisses placed everywhere, and when their desires could no longer be contained, the many ways they'd made love as the water rained down from the large overhead and side showerheads. Alexander's hand moved toward his crotch, only to have the sexual train of thought broken by the ringing of his cell phone.

"Dammit, man…what are you doing?" he chastised, adjusting himself in his pants. Alexander walked out of China's bedroom and back downstairs. He pulled out his phone and hit Redial. "What's up?"

"What's up with you?" Brice asked. "I heard how you carried China out of here. Pulling *An Officer and a Gentleman* move after all these weeks. Well, that's one way to go, I guess."

"A what?"

"You know, like in the movie," Brice explained.

"You really need to get out more, man. Sitting around watching old movies is definitely something you get from our mother."

"Actually, my soon-to-be ex hooked me on that one, but that's another story."

"What do you want, Brice?" Alexander knew his annoyance was coming through loud and clear.

"I want to know what's going on with China—with you and China, actually."

"Nothing. She got that stomach virus that's knocked everybody on their asses and she was too sick to be at work, so I brought her home. That's it," he explained.

"Yikes, I know how she feels, too. But to get her home you had to carry her from the office, onto the elevator, down forty-eight floors and into your waiting car—how very romantic."

"If you didn't call me for any reason other than to harass me, I have to go. I'm going to see if Mom will have her doctor call something in for China's nausea. You know China won't go see her own doctor until she's tried the wait-and-see-if-it-passes strategy first."

"Okay…okay. I do have a small piece of business to discuss with you."

"Make it quick," Alexander spat back.

"James Pauls, our quality control manager, recently requested a new set of access cards. Cards that get him into the building at night and even onto the executive floors," Brice informed Alexander.

"What happened to his old set?"

"He claims he lost them."

"Claims? James has been with us for years. He has no reason to try and hurt us," Alexander defended their longtime employee.

"We have to check everyone," Brice reminded Alexander.

"I know, and he's already on the list. I'll let you know when I set the meeting with Montgomery."

"Cool. By the way, ask Gregory to hook China up with some of his homemade soups—chicken noodle or rice. She'll want something heartier when this thing starts to pass. I should know."

"Good idea, but I don't need Gregory for that." Alexander's confidence in his cooking was on full display.

"Yeah, you do," Brice said, laughing. "Later."

Alexander hung up from his brother, dialed his mother to put in one of the two suggested requests as he reached for the door.

China sat on her bathroom chaise wrapped in a towel. She hadn't lied when she told Alexander that she felt a little better, but now she felt as if she was suffering the effects of a really bad or really good night of partying; her body ached and her head was swimming. "Pull it together, China," she instructed her wet reflection in the bathroom mirror.

She stood slowly, dried herself off and walked into her closet. China opened a drawer in the large marble-and-wood island placed in the middle of the expansive room. She bypassed her normal nightwear in favor of something comfortable and a little more fun: her favorite comic book character pajamas. Although she certainly didn't feel like a powerful Amazon warrior at the moment.

China put on the oversize white robe that Victoria had insisted on buying her on one of their many shopping trips. She wrapped her still-wet hair up in a large towel, hoping it would soak up the remaining water. China grabbed one of her light blankets and made her way downstairs.

Before her feet hit the last step she noticed her security system had been set. She folded her arms across her chest like a wounded child. "So much for taking care of me," she murmured. China realized she was being unreasonable, but she didn't care. Her mind knew Alexander had done the right thing by leaving. His close presence only brought her more confusion, yet her heart ached to be near him.

China entered her living room and immediately noticed a plate of dry toast, a bottle of ginger ale and an empty glass. She dropped her arms and sighed. "Oh, Alex." She reached for the piece of toast, sat on the sofa wrapped in her blanket and turned on the movie she hadn't finished the night before. She set the remote on the table and opened the ginger ale. Forgoing the glass, China took several sips from the bottle. After propping up her pillow, she lay on her right side and started watching the movie. "Go get them, Denzel."

After nearly an hour had passed, China heard her front door open. She used her hands to push herself up and into a seated position. She had learned the hard way what quick movements could do to her stomach. Turning her body to face the door, China could see Alexander disarming her alarm. He held two large grocery bags and a small white one that appeared to have come from the pharmacy. Alexander locked the door and walked into the living room. He came to stand behind the sofa, saying, "Good, you're resting. What are you watching?"

"Denzel Washington's *Equalizer*," she replied, smiling up at him.

"That's my girl." Alexander slid the back of his right hand down the side of her face; she shivered and her heart sped up.

"What's all that?" China stood slowly.

"Groceries. You have nothing in your refrigerator but leftover takeout—that needed to be tossed days ago, by the way. Sit down, I'll put everything away and make us something to eat," he ordered, walking into her kitchen.

China followed him. "I'm fine. I'm on the downside of this thing."

Alexander watched as she swayed and gingerly sat down. With a raised left eyebrow, he mockingly said, "Really?"

"Okay, maybe I haven't made it to the other side to start going down it yet, but I can certainly sit here and watch you make dinner."

"Just like old times."

China leveled her eyes on him. "I miss those times. I especially miss our monthly dinners where you tried to convince me that you were the next Iron Chef."

Alexander smirked. "I miss them, too."

Alexander and China stared at each other for several moments. China realized in that instant that her relationship with Alexander had been forever changed. Things between them felt comfortable and familiar, yet new all at the same time. Now they just had to figure out how to manage this new relationship moving forward.

"So, what are you making us?" she asked.

"Brice thinks that, as you start to get better, you'll want something of more substance to eat."

"Well, he did have this thing a couple weeks ago, so he would know. So…"

"So what?" he asked as he put the groceries away.

"What are you going to make?"

"I was thinking about my chicken and mushroom rice dinner. You love that," he reminded her, smiling.

China frowned and patted her stomach. "I do, but I don't think I'm ready for that yet. Maybe something a little tamer."

"Like what?"

"How about—"

The doorbell interrupted her requests. "Hold that thought. I'll get the door," he offered.

China slid out of the booth. "This is my house, remember. Why don't you figure out what you're going to make for dinner that won't have me relapsing even before I'm well?" she teased, heading out of the room. China opened the door and her eyes widened.

Jackson stood smiling down at her. He was wearing green scrubs and tennis shoes, and was holding a bag from her favorite deli. "Hello, lovely lady," he said, gifting her with a wide smile.

"Jackson, what are you doing here?"

Jackson's smile quickly faded. "Is this a bad time?" he asked, looking past China into the house.

China could sense she was no longer alone in her foyer. "No, Jackson, this isn't a bad time."

Chapter 11

"Would you like to come in?" China offered, stepping aside.

"Only for a moment. I have to get back to the hospital," Jackson explained. His eyes darted between China and a menacing-looking Alexander.

"Pardon my manners. Jackson Weatherly, this is my best friend and boss, Alexander Kingsley. I may have mentioned him a time or two," she said on a nervous laugh.

"Yes, of course." Jackson extended his hand to Alexander. "Pleased to meet you."

"And you," Alexander said, accepting his hand and giving it a firm but quick shake before folding his arms across his chest. He stood back and leaned against the stair railing.

Jackson turned his back to Alexander, giving China his full attention. "I wasn't sure if you would be ready to eat much of anything yet, but since we both know you barely keep enough food in this house to feed an invisible pet, I thought you should have something here just in case you did." He handed her the bag.

China smiled. "Thank you, Jackson, that's very sweet of you."

"I'm a sweet man." Jackson flashed a toothy smile.

"That you are," she agreed, her eyes colliding with Alexander's as he stood by quietly. She could see the muscles in his jaw tighten. China felt like a heel for being more worried about how Alexander was feeling than the handsome man standing in front of her. The man she was contemplating having a child with.

"I should go. Nice meeting you," Jackson said to Alexander, who replied with a nod. Jackson took China's hand and walked toward the door.

"Oh, wait, your watch is upstairs. I can go get it."

"I trust you. I'll get it later. Can I call you when I leave the hospital?" he asked.

"Of course."

China closed the door behind Jackson, took a deep, cleansing breath and slowly turned to face Alexander, only he'd left the room. She walked into the kitchen, placed the food at the end of the island and took a seat. It was the only area where Alexander wasn't feverishly chopping up onions and celery.

"What are you doing?" she asked, pulling containers out of the warming bag.

"I'm putting my chicken on. I've decided to make chicken and dumplings."

"Sounds good." China opened the lid to one of the two containers and took a whiff.

"What did your boy bring you?" he questioned, dropping his cut vegetables and chicken into a pot of boiling water before lowering the flame.

"Soup—tomato and basil in this one." China replaced the lid and moved to the other container. "And this one is chicken and rice."

Alexander reached into the cabinet and pulled out a bowl and handed it to China. "You should probably eat while it's hot."

China removed a ladle and spoon from her utensil drawer. "I guess that means you won't be joining me."

Alexander gave China the side eye as he reached for his vibrating phone. He sent the caller to voice mail. "I'll pass." Alexander opened the refrigerator, pulled out a bottle of ginger ale and handed it to China before retrieving the premade dough and the flour he'd bought. "I never understood why you keep flour in the refrigerator."

"My mom always said it was the best way to keep flour fresh and bug-free," she said.

"Bug-free?" Alexander frowned.

"Mom always told me that you should keep flour and sugar in the refrigerator so bugs can't get inside the bags," she explained, offering up a weak smile. China suddenly felt overwhelmed by sadness. No matter how hard it might have been growing up with a mother so much older than all the other mothers, she adored her, and China especially missed her when she was sick. China's mother taught her many things that she couldn't wait to share with her own children.

Alexander could see the tears China was trying not to shed. He knew what a loving but complicated relationship China and her mother had had, and that it was driving her desperate need to become a mother at a much younger age. Alexander reached into the cabinet for another bowl. While he really didn't want to eat anything that Jackson provided, Alexander knew China would appreciate it. He opened the refrigerator and pulled out a Coke. He grabbed a soup spoon, came around the island and took a seat next to China.

China smiled. "Changed your mind."

"I figure I shouldn't let you eat alone. Besides, my food won't be ready for another hour."

"Think of it as an appetizer." China picked up both containers. "Tomato or chicken and rice?"

"I'll try the tomato."

"Me, too." China ladled up both bowls.

"What's the deal with this guy? How'd you two meet?" Alexander asked, bringing the spoon to his mouth. He had been determined not to ask anything about Jackson but he couldn't help himself.

"Do you really want to talk about Jackson?" China held his gaze.

"Not really, but if he's going to be a part of your life and we are friends, I think I should know a little bit about him other than the fact that he has excellent taste in watches," he said, gifting her with a lopsided grin.

China giggled. "That's right. You have one, too."

"Three, actually, but back to you and Jackson. How *did* you meet him?"

"Well, if you really want to know…"

"I do." Alexander braced himself for whatever she was about to say because he knew whatever it was could shatter his heart.

"We met through More Than Just Dating."

"That cheesy dating website that caters to the rich and privileged?" Alexander couldn't hide his surprise.

"More Than Just Dating is different. It's not just a dating website," she defended it.

"How so?" Alexander retrieved a box of crackers from the pantry.

"It brings people together for specific reasons."

"Like…" he prompted, crumbling crackers into his soup.

China laughed. "I see you still think crackers should be a seasoning or a garnish for your soup."

Alexander watched China dip her crackers in her bowl. "And I see you still think soup is a dip for yours."

China laughed. "Forget you."

"So, tell me what makes this website so different. What was your specific reason for going to them, or need I even ask?"

"Probably not. People seek help from their agency when they want to cut through all the crap. Some want to find long-term partners, some want marriage and some want sperm donors."

"Sperm donors?" Alexander asked, stopping the spoon before it reached his mouth.

"Yes, but the difference here is that you have the option to meet the donor and even develop a relationship, if you like."

Alexander put his spoon down and his eyes scanned China's face. "Is that what Jackson is to you, a potential sperm donor?"

China took a drink of her soda. "I haven't decided what Jackson is to me yet."

Alexander felt as if he'd just been hit in the gut. Was it the idea that China had actually moved forward with her plans to become a mother, or that she was doing so with another man? He fought the emotions that were building and said, "I know you, China. You don't go into anything without a plan."

"When I first signed up with More Than Just Dating, I didn't know what path I was going to take. Then I met

Jackson, and the idea of traveling the road to parenthood with a partner became more attractive." China sighed.

In that moment, Alexander realized that he could actually lose China. He felt as if the air had been sucked out of the room. "I see."

"Jackson is successful in his own right, so my success isn't intimidating. He wants a family just as much as I do and he's a really sweet man. If you give him a chance, I think you'd really like him. You might even become friends."

Alexander folded his arms across his chest to stop himself from reaching out and shaking some sense into China for thinking this was a path she should take or that he'd actually be friends with the man trying to take her away from him. "You think so?"

China raised both eyebrows. "Yes, I do. That is, if you meant it when you said we'd be friends no matter what," she reminded him.

"I did and *we* will." Alexander went to check on his food. "This needs to simmer but should be ready in about another thirty minutes. How do you feel?"

"Better, actually."

"Good." Alexander started cleaning the kitchen. He needed to move, to get his blood flowing and his lungs working normally again. He felt like he'd been holding his breath throughout the entire conversation.

"You don't have to do that, you know."

"I know," he said, loading the dishwasher.

"So...are you seeing anyone?" China asked, running her index finger along the rim of her soda bottle.

Alexander stopped wringing out the sponge he held and smiled. The tone of her voice told him China was more than just curious and it was like the sun had been let into a dark room. He put the sponge on its resting place and turned to face China. "Not at the moment."

"I know what that means." China slid off the stool and walked into the living room, where she picked up the remote and lay down on her couch.

"You think so?" he said, following her.

"Yep, it means you're juggling more than one woman and you aren't serious about either of them, like always."

Now is as good a time as any. "Actually, China—"

China's house phone rang, interrupting Alexander. The caller's name popped up on the television screen. "Jackson," she murmured.

"I can see that. I'll let you take your call. You stay home until you're feeling better. That's an order. I'll lock up on my way out."

"Thanks, Alex, for everything."

Alexander acknowledged her thank-you with a nod before walking out the door. "Hello, Jackson" was the last thing he heard.

Alexander stood outside China's house, fighting hard not to go back inside and claim China as his own, demand that she give them a chance. But to do that, he'd have to address his concerns and fears of becoming a parent, and that wasn't something he was prepared to do. However, he'd meant it when he said they'd be friends no matter what, so he had to respect her choices; he just hadn't expected it to be so difficult. Alexander had tried being aloof and businesslike with China and it nearly drove him insane. Now he figured he'd try a novel approach: getting back to their real friendship. Yet he knew there was no way in hell he would be Jackson's friend.

"Time to find our company's Judas," he said out loud, knowing that work would be the perfect distraction from his feelings for China. Alexander pulled out his cell phone and returned the call he'd been waiting for.

"Meeks Montgomery…"

"Good evening, Mr. Montgomery, this is Alexander Kingsley. I appreciate you returning my phone call."

"Please call me Meeks. What can I do for you?"

"I have some company business, as well as a personal matter I'd like to discuss with you." *It wouldn't hurt to have Jackson Weatherly checked out. What are friends for?*

Chapter 12

After being forced by the entire Kingsley clan to take a few days off and while she still wasn't quite herself, China felt much better and was looking forward to finally getting back to work. She walked into Alexander's office to find an attractive, fair-skinned woman wearing a bright pink, scoop-neck blouse sitting behind his desk and typing on Alexander's computer.

"Excuse me, may I help you with something?" China asked, her cell phone in hand ready to call for security.

"Well, it is Monday morning and I could use a cup of coffee. Make it two. I'm sure Alex will want one too when he comes back," the strange woman said, not bothering to look up from what she was doing.

"Alex?"

"That's right, you people call him Alexander. I keep forgetting that." She shook her head, as if that was unbelievable.

"Who—?"

"China," a familiar voice called from behind her. "Good morning. It's good to see that you're back at work. I hope you're feeling better. I see you've met Wednesday."

"Wednesday?" China frowned. "No, we haven't met. Yet she thinks I should be fetching you two coffees… Alex," she said, giving him the evil eye. China couldn't keep her irritation under wraps.

"Done!" Wednesday said excitedly, before turning the chair to face her audience. "And you are?"

"Wondering who the hell you think you are," China said, moving closer to the desk.

"Allow me to make the proper introductions," Alexander said as he came to fill the space between the two women. "China Edwards, this is Wednesday Adams. She's a security expert and private investigator for Blake & Montgomery." Alexander gestured toward China with his right hand. "Wednesday, China is our in-house counsel."

"Wednesday Adams?" Doubt laced China's words.

Wednesday rose, pressed down her white pencil skirt and offered her hand. "My parents had a sick obsession with the Addams Family. Pleased to meet you." China accepted her hand, giving it a quick shake. "Forgive my—"

"Rudeness…" China supplied.

"Yes, I get tunnel vision when I'm working. Speaking of which—" Wednesday sat back down and turned to the computer "—you're up and ready to go."

"That was fast," Alexander replied, moving to stand behind Wednesday. He leaned forward and said, "Show me what you've done."

China suddenly felt out of place, lightheaded and even a bit warm in her short-sleeved flower-print dress. She took a seat in a chair across from the desk and angled it so she could see the screen. "What are we looking at?"

"Are you okay?" Alexander asked, his forehead creased. "You sure you didn't come back to work too soon?"

Not soon enough. "I'm fine," China reassured him, fanning herself with her hand.

Wednesday turned her head toward China. "Alex…I mean, Alexander told me you'd been out sick. I'm glad you're okay." She lifted her head, looked over her shoulder and met Alexander's gaze. "Sorry, I forgot 'Alex' is a private thing."

"No worries, China's a friend."

The way Alexander said her name and "friend" in that sentence was like a stab in the heart. It literally made China sick. "Excuse me."

She ran to Alexander's private bathroom, where she lost what little breakfast she'd managed to keep down that morning. She washed her face and brushed her teeth with the same toothbrush she'd used several weeks ago. China liked seeing her toothbrush still hanging in a holder next to Alexander's. She knew it was a silly thought, but it made her feel special. China looked in the mirror and swiped away a long tear. "What the hell's wrong with you?" she asked her reflection. China washed and dried her hands before opening the bathroom door to find a concerned-looking Alexander standing waiting for her.

"Are you all right, China?" he asked.

"Aren't you tired of asking me that question? Yes, of course." She walked around him and returned to her seat.

"You don't look all right. I thought you were over that bug." He sounded doubtful as he walked behind her.

"I am…mostly."

"Alexander, some viruses are harder to shake than others," Wednesday offered, standing next to his desk.

"Are you a doctor, too, Wednesday?" China asked, glaring at Wednesday.

"No, but I played one, once," she said, laughing.

Alexander released a boisterous laugh and China forced a small smile. "Funny. Can we get back to business? Tell me what's ready to go." Wednesday looked at Alexander as if she was waiting for permission to share their secret. Alexander nodding to give that permission only irritated China more. "Well…"

Wednesday sat behind Alexander's desk again. "I've installed an application that will allow Alexander, and whomever he assigns, to follow the investigation in real time," she explained as she clicked the mouse and brought up what appeared to be a page where a report would appear. She reached into her pink Chanel bag, pulled out her phone and spoke into it. "Security check complete. Client demonstration under way." As she spoke, her dictation appeared on the screen and in the report.

"Very nice," Alexander replied.

"If photos are taken, they, too, will be attached to the report," she informed them.

"Show me," Alexander requested, his face lit up with excitement.

Wednesday came around the desk to stand next to Alexander. She stood so close to him that China couldn't tell where he began and she ended. China couldn't believe that she was actually jealous of the woman. Wednesday held the camera out, took a selfie of the two of them, and within seconds it appeared on the screen. "Satisfied?"

"Very," he said, offering Wednesday a wide smile.

"Exactly what other services will you be providing?" China asked, knowing that she was probably coming across as catty, but she didn't care.

Alexander frowned. "Well—"

"I asked Wednesday," China snapped back at Alexander. "After all, I am lead counsel. I'd hate for us to get into more trouble trying to get out of it." China turned her attention to Wednesday. "I'm sure you understand."

"I certainly do," Wednesday reassured her.

Alexander's eyes darted between both women. "Let's all have a seat and, Wednesday, you can share the plan with China," Alexander suggested.

"Sure." Wednesday turned toward the computer.

"Wednesday, why don't you take the chair next to me?" China directed, patting the chair's arm. "I think we've seen enough for now. Let's let Alexander have his desk and chair back, shall we?"

Alexander wordlessly took his seat, as did Wednesday. She settled in her chair and crossed her long legs. "Shall I start at the top?" She directed her question to Alexander.

China rolled her eyes at the exchange. "Please do," Alexander said.

Wednesday spent the next hour outlining how Blake & Montgomery's operations worked, the upgrades they'd made to the current security systems of Kingsley Oil and Gas, as well as the detailed plan to find the whistle-blower.

"Well, if anyone can help us find this person, I'm sure you and your team can," Alexander offered with a great deal of confidence.

"Thank you." Wednesday checked her watch. "I have another appointment but I'll see you later. I wish everyone a good day. Walk me out." She picked up her purse and waited for Alexander to rise.

Alexander walked Wednesday to the door. "What time should I expect you tonight?"

"It may be close to nine," she stated.

"No problem."

"Nice meeting you, China. I hope you continue to feel better," Wednesday said, waving over her shoulder as she walked out.

* * *

Alexander closed the door and turned to find China standing with her arms folded across her breasts. She had a deep frown on her face and most of her weight on her right leg. He recognized the stance immediately; it usually came before they were about to have a big fight. *Some things will never change.*

"What's wrong, China?" Alexander walked back to his desk, sat down and started signing documents.

China turned and stared down at him. "What's wrong? How could you move forward with this without talking to me first?"

"About what…hiring Blake & Montgomery?" he questioned, his forehead crumpled.

"Yes. You said you were going to schedule something so we could all meet with them together."

"I did, but you weren't available Friday and everyone else was, so we moved forward," he explained, shrugging.

"Oh, so, by 'everyone,' you meant your family. I get it." China dropped her hands and her head slightly, and turned to leave.

Alexander came from around his desk to stand in front of China so fast he barely remembered his feet touching the ground. "Stop…please." He grabbed China by the shoulders with both hands. "You know I didn't mean it like that." Alexander released her shoulders and used both hands to cup China's face. "Look at me."

China released a breath and slowly raised her head. She opened her eyes. Alexander could see the tears as they began to fall and his heart sank. "No matter what or who comes into our lives, we will always be each other's family, understand?"

China nodded. Alexander used the pads of his thumbs to wipe away her tears. He dropped his hands and took a step back before he lost all the friendship ground he'd gained, because all he wanted to do was kiss her into submission.

"Sorry, this nausea medicine has my emotions all over the place," China explained.

"You still taking them?"

"Off and on. It seems this bug doesn't want to let me go."

"I can understand that," he whispered. Alexander couldn't help himself, he just had to touch her. He held her gaze as he ran his thumb across her lips and took a step forward. It was like he was being drawn to her by a magnet.

"Wednesday seems qualified, and she's very attractive," China said.

Alexander sighed and dropped his hand. *Friend zone.* "That she is, on both fronts," he said, returning to his desk.

"So, where do we go from here?"

Alexander looked up at China and said, "Back to work."

Chapter 13

For the rest of the day and into the evening, China was at her desk, going over every piece of material she could find, trying to determine how an incorrect procedure could have made it through all their safeguards. "Dammit." She dropped her pencil and rubbed her eyes.

"Still coming up empty?" Joyce asked, entering the office carrying a brown bag and two drinks.

"Unfortunately, yes."

"Well, let's fortify ourselves before we take another crack at it." Joyce handed China a cup. "Here's a chocolate shake for you and strawberry for me."

China took a long pull through her straw. "Hmm... delicious," she said. "What did you get us to eat?"

"Hamburgers and fries from Jax's, of course." Joyce handed China a basket that held her medium-well burger and fries before taking a seat and pulling out her medium-rare one. "I can't understand why people eat their meat well-done in any form."

China smiled and took a big bite. "This is so good," she said with her hand over her mouth.

"I'm just glad you can finally eat."

"Me, too. I just hope it lasts," she said, before taking another bite of her burger.

"So, where were we before I left to get dinner?" Joyce popped a fry into her mouth.

China wiped her lips. "We received the EPA's specs on the proper disposal of gas cylinders." She placed her right hand on a white binder that sat on the right side of her desk.

"And we submitted and received approval for our plans for implementing our disposal procedures based off those specs," Joyce added.

"Yes." China placed her left hand on a stack of documents that lay in front of her. "And we took those approved plans, entered them in our system and implemented the process."

"Yet the plans we're following today are incorrect. It's as if the correct ones magically disappeared from the system, somehow."

"Magically disappeared," China murmured. "That's it." China pushed her half-eaten meal to the side and reached for a stack of files that had been placed in the center of her desk.

"What are you looking for, and are you done with that?" Joyce pointed at China's food.

"Yes," she said, laughing at Joyce, who had already reached for the burger before China got the reply out of her mouth. "I'm looking for Mr. Lee's written log, because I remember seeing something."

"His what?"

China reached for her shake and took a drink. "Mr. Lee

keeps a log of every package that's delivered to the mailroom for anyone on the executive team."

"Why? Wait, I have a better question for you. He's like one hundred years old—why is he still working here?" Joyce's nose crinkled.

"Mr. Lee is seventy-five, actually, and he works because he wants to and not because he has to, trust me," China informed her friend with raised eyebrows.

Joyce opened the lid of her cup and took a big gulp of her shake. "What does that mean?"

"Mr. Lee didn't always work in the mailroom. According to Alexander, he handled special projects for Alexander Senior, and when he died, Mr. Lee was one of the first people to pledge his loyalty to Victoria when she took over as CEO."

"Wow…"

"I know."

Joyce frowned. "But why the demotion…and to the mailroom, of all places?"

"According to Alexander, he wanted to leave his old job but he wasn't ready to retire, so they let him decide where he wanted to go. He picked the mailroom."

"That's cool."

"Yeah and in return, the Kingsleys have taken care of him and his whole family."

Joyce scratched her head. "I wonder what special projects he performed for them."

"Feel free to ask Victoria the next time you see her."

Joyce rolled her eyes. "So, what does his log have to do with this case?"

"When a package comes in for any executive, Mr. Lee tracks it. It's tagged with a number and logged in. Here we go." China opened a thin blue binder and ran her finger down several pages before she said, "Yes!"

"What did you find?"

"Two days after we heard verbally that our plans were approved, the EPA's official authorization and all the appropriate documents were delivered. Those plans were logged in as received and should have been entered into our secure quality control system, like always. According to this—" China pointed to a line on a page in the blue binder "—twenty-four hours later, there was a second package delivered from the EPA."

"For the same set of plans? Maybe it was just another copy," Joyce offered as she brought another French fry to her mouth.

"That's a good question." China ran her fingers across her computer keyboard.

"What are you doing?" Joyce questioned, as she began collecting the trash from their food and dumping it into China's garbage can.

"Whenever documents are scanned into the system, they create a folder where all copies associated with that scan are kept. If there were two entries, there should be two folders with separate sets of documents. Even if the second set of documents was a duplicate, they'd still be placed in the system. Only one set should indicate that they were duplicates or that there was some type of error. I'm checking the archives for the scanned documents now."

"What would that mean for the EPA's claim?"

China sneered. "If two sets of documents were entered, one right and one wrong, we would have a strong case for some type of administrative error. Here we go."

"And…"

"And there's only one entry, and it's for the initial package of documents and approvals we received that matches what's on the written log."

"That's good."

China shook her head. "No, it's not. The only documents listed as coming from that initial package are the ones currently in use today."

Joyce frowned. "The ones we *shouldn't* be using."

"Right," China confirmed.

"How is that possible?"

"Someone had to have manipulated the system. After the correct documents had been received and entered, someone entered the system and switched them, covering their tracks in the process. Only the written log shows that we received two separate deliveries, and the EPA could argue that we forged that second entry, especially if they can show that they only sent the one," China explained.

"Whoever changed it must not know about Mr. Lee's written log," Joyce suggested.

"That or…"

"Or what?" Joyce asked, frowning.

"Or they didn't change it to knock us off our guard," China speculated.

"Who could have removed it?" Joyce wondered out loud as she watched China search the computer access log. "This is a secure server and only a handful of people have access to it."

China stared at the access code used, recognizing it immediately. She turned in her chair to face her assistant. "According to the system, it was Alexander."

"Knock, knock…you ready?" Wednesday asked, walking into Alexander's office. She was wearing a fitted Houston Carriers jersey, blue jeans and stilettos. "I certainly am."

Alexander sat back in his chair and smiled as he admired Wednesday's outfit, but not for the reason she might think. It reminded him of something China would wear, only she wouldn't dare wear stilettos to an NBA basketball game, especially his brother's. "That you are. Just let me log off my system and put these papers away."

Alexander had started stacking his files when Tammy entered the office. "Oh, wow, Wednesday, don't you look ready for the game."

"Thank you, Tammy. I love basketball."

"You two go. I'll take care of that," Tammy said to Alexander, waving her hand in front of his desk. "After all, I am your assistant."

"I thought you were leaving, too. Don't you and Sam have dinner plans?"

"No, he got called in to work. I'm going to catch up on a few things here and he'll pick me up for a late dinner," Tammy explained as she straightened the files on Alexander's desk.

"That's romantic," Wednesday volunteered.

"Yeah, he does that a lot," Tammy said, admiring her engagement ring."

"Nice ring. May I?" Wednesday asked, offering her palm.

"Of course." Tammy proudly presented her left hand in order for Wednesday to get a closer look.

Women and diamonds, this could take forever. "Well, if you really don't mind putting everything away, I'd really appreciate it. I guess we can take off," Alexander said, ushering a smiling Wednesday toward the door.

Tammy waved and said, "Have fun, you two."

Alexander led Wednesday out of the office to the elevator, where he pushed the down button and stood silently, waiting for the car to arrive. "I hope Tammy knows that diamond is man-made," she murmured.

"Sam gave Tammy a fake diamond...you sure?"

Wednesday looked at Alexander as if she didn't recognize him. "Of course I'm sure. I know diamonds."

"I'm sure there's a perfectly good explanation for it." Alexander hoped so, anyway.

"Are you going to say something?" she asked.

"No, I don't want to embarrass anyone. If she needs me, I'm here."

Wednesday nodded. "So, how long has Tammy worked for you?"

"About three years for me, but nine years for the company," he said.

"She's our age. So, what, is this her first real job?"

"As a matter of fact, it is. She worked part-time while in school and was hired full-time after graduation. Why?"

Wednesday shrugged and said, "Just curious if she and China were close."

His jaw clinched. "I guess, but what does it matter, and why all the questions?"

"Just wondering how long it will be before she calls and tells China that you're taking me to the game."

"What makes you think China would even care? She may be my best friend but she has her own personal life. She's seeing someone, actually."

Wednesday smirked. "You didn't see the way she looked at me before you came in this morning."

"You're reading something into nothing. She was just surprised to see someone sitting behind the desk in my private office, is all." The door to the elevator opened and Alexander waved Wednesday forward so she could enter ahead of him. "Especially someone she didn't know."

Alexander hit the button for the garage and they started to descend. "If you say so, but I know a woman's possessive look when I see one." Wednesday shifted her weight to her right foot. "How often do you get to see your brother play?"

Before Alexander could reply, the elevator stopped on the forty-eighth floor and the doors opened to China and Joyce. "Good evening, ladies," Alexander said, smiling as he stepped to the side of the car, away from Wednesday.

"This should be interesting," Wednesday murmured.

"Good evening, Alexander," Joyce replied, while China simply smiled and offered a short nod.

Alexander watched China as she kept her eyes on the descending numbers. He couldn't help but notice how she was gripping the handle of her purse and how the temperature in the elevator car seemed to drop with each floor they passed.

"KJ's in town," Alexander informed her in an effort to bring the warmth back to the space. China and KJ had a close, brother–sister type relationship, and he hoped a reminder of that would ease the tension between the two of them.

A corner of China's mouth rose and she released her grip on her Louis Vuitton handbag. "Please send my love to KJ," China said, keeping her eyes on the elevator panel.

"How long will he be in town?" Joyce asked.

"Two days," he said.

China's phone rang and she pulled it out of an inside compartment of her bag. She looked at the screen and smiled, but sent the caller to voice mail before dropping her phone haphazardly into her purse. It was a move that didn't go unnoticed by Alexander and he knew who the caller had to have been. He fisted his hands at his sides but remained quiet.

"Well, if he has time, please tell him to stop by the office," Joyce requested. "We miss him around here."

"Will do," Alexander promised.

The elevator came to a stop and the doors opened to Alexander's waiting vehicle. China turned her head toward Alexander. "Have fun," she said, before exiting the elevator.

"Have a good evening," Joyce said, following China.

Alexander walked Wednesday to the passenger side of his car and opened the door. She stood between the door and the car and said, "Oh, yeah. She not only cares, but it seems like you care, too."

"I don't know what you mean," he defended himself.

"I saw your face when China sent that call, from who I can only assume was her man, to voice mail. Anything you'd like to share?"

Alexander went poker-faced. "I don't know what you thought you saw, but there's nothing going on between me and China other than friendship."

Wednesday got into the car. "If you say so," she replied, her disbelief clear.

Alexander closed the door and walked around the car, murmuring, "I say so."

Chapter 14

"Good morning, Brice. You got a minute?" China asked, standing in his office doorway. Between the information she'd found in the system implicating duplicity on Alexander's part and seeing him and Wednesday heading out for their date, China had a restless night and really needed to talk to her best friend.

Brice was in front of his new vertical desk that had been placed on the left side of the traditional mahogany desk that sat in the middle of his office, directly in front of his wall of windows.

"For you, anytime," he said, waving her forward. "Don't you look nice."

China looked down at the royal blue silk Diane von Furstenberg sheath dress and matching heels she got from Cheap Rack and smiled. *I have to thank Joyce for hooking me up with that store—brand-name clothes at reasonable prices.* No matter how successful she was, China still liked her deals. "Thanks, so do you."

"It's hard not to look decent in a simple blue suit," he rebutted her words.

"Givenchy doesn't make anything simple," she said, laughing. "I see your new desk has arrived. How is it?" China's enthusiasm was on full display.

"It's great, and so much better for your back," he informed her.

"I know, and I can't wait until mine comes in." Her eyes sparkled.

"What's up?"

"I figured out how the bogus plans got in our system and I want to talk to Alexander about it. Have you seen him? He's not answering my calls and Tammy's not in yet," China explained, frowning.

"Tammy called out sick and Alexander is at a breakfast meeting with Wednesday." Brice tilted his head and squinted his eyes as if he was studying her face.

"Oh…"

"I'm not sure why he's not taking your calls right now, but I bet there's a good explanation." Brice lifted his left eyebrow. "It's not like you haven't sent his calls to voice mail a time or two."

China crossed her arms and sat in one of the large round chairs in front of his desk, trying hard not to look like a petulant child. "True, but I actually call him back in a timely manner."

"And I'm sure eventually he'll call you, as well. Until then, care to tell me what you found?"

It was as if China hadn't heard a word he said. She continued, "I bet you think I'm being ridiculous considering—"

"Considering you're in a relationship with someone else," Brice stated, giving her a curious stare.

China sat up in her chair. "Jackson and I are not in a relationship...exactly. We're just two good friends getting to know each other better," she enlightened him, with a little more force than she'd intended.

"Like you and my brother." Brice's expression was deadpan.

Nothing compared to what she and Alexander had. "Not at all," she murmured, staring down at her hands.

"What did you figure out?" Clearly Brice was ready to change the subject, which suited her just fine. China raised her head to find that Brice had moved to the stationary desk. "Looks like our gas cylinder disposal procedures were entered correctly initially. Only someone changed them."

"What do you mean?"

China explained what she and Joyce discovered the previous night and the implications. "You know Alexander didn't make that change," Brice insisted.

"Of course he didn't, but we have to find out who did, because the way it looks right now, this could go a long way in supporting the EPA's claim. Not to mention what it could do to Alexander."

Brice hit the speaker button on his phone and started dialing. "Who are you calling?"

"We need to get Wednesday and her team on this right away."

China briefly looked heavenward. "Wednesday..." She watched as amusement crossed Brice's face. "Did I say that out loud?"

The corners of Brice's mouth turned up. "Yep."

China sank back into her chair. "Hello," a familiar baritone voice said through the phone.

"Alexander, there's been a development. How soon will you be in the office?"

"We just arrived," Alexander replied.

"We…" China said.

"Is that China?" Alexander asked.

"Yes. See you in a few." Brice disconnected the call.

China got to her feet and was suddenly hit with a wave of vertigo. "Whoa." She sat back down.

"You okay, China?"

"Yeah, I'm fine. It's just this bug is hanging around a little longer than I expected."

Brice retrieved a bottle of water from his minirefrigerator and handed it to her. "That forty-eight-hour virus I had has hung around you nearly a week. You might need to get that checked out," he suggested.

"If it hasn't passed in a few more days, I will…promise. But do me a favor and don't say anything to Alex—you know how he can get."

"I do, he gets like me. We're brothers. Remember, to us you're family, so we worry about you, too."

China smiled and nodded. Brice was right; the Kingsleys had always treated her like family and she prayed that would never change. "If I'm not better by the weekend, I'll go to the doctor. You have my word."

"Brice, darling." Victoria walked into Brice's office wearing all white. He hugged and kissed his mother on both cheeks, the only method of welcome acceptable to her.

"Mother, what are you doing here?"

"I told you, we had that breakfast meeting with Wednesday and the rest of the Blake & Montgomery team," Alexander explained, stepping into the office behind his mother.

"Good morning, China, darling." Victoria pulled China, who was now standing next to Brice, into a hug.

"Good morning, Victoria," China replied.

Once she was released from Victoria's grip, China's eyes bored into Brice. "What?" he asked, smirking.

"You know what." China poked Brice in the side with her elbow.

Alexander observed this strange exchange between China and his brother but before he could inquire as to what was going on, Wednesday's appearance changed the atmosphere, which had Brice and China retreating to their respective corners.

"My apologies—that call took a little longer than I expected," Wednesday explained, dropping her cell phone into her purse.

"Now that we're all here, why don't you tell us what's going on, China?" Victoria instructed, taking a seat behind Brice's desk. Victoria looked over at Brice and said, "You don't mind, do you, dear? You prefer to stand while you work nowadays, right?"

"Of course I don't mind, Mother," he reassured Victoria.

Both Wednesday and China took seats facing Victoria, while Alexander and Brice stood in front of his vertical desk. "Well...?" Victoria encouraged China with an open hand.

China released a breath and began to explain what she'd discovered and the implications of that discovery if taken at face value.

"Wait. My access codes were used?" Alexander asked, taking a step forward.

"Yes," China replied.

"Not possible. You must have made a mistake," he accused her.

China stood and turned to face Alexander. She raised

her chin and placed her hands on her hips. "I don't make mistakes," she defended herself.

Alexander placed his hands in his pockets and stared down at China. "Oh, really? I seem to recall a couple of mistakes you've made lately. After all, you have been distracted with your personal life." China recoiled at the statement. Alexander knew he was being petty, but he knew he couldn't see past his own hurt and anger. They stood glaring at each other.

"My money's on China," Brice offered, garnering an angry stare from his mother.

"That's enough, you two," Victoria said, her tone sharp.

China dropped her hands and went to stand on the opposite side of the room. It was clear that she needed to put some space between herself and Alexander.

Victoria turned her attention to Wednesday. "You have to excuse this little outburst and show of disrespect. As you can imagine, we're all upset about what's happened and very passionate about what we do."

"They're certainly passionate about something," Wednesday concluded.

"What do you think this discovery could mean?" Victoria asked Wednesday.

"There could be a number of different explanations as to how this could have happened that have nothing to do with Alexander," Wednesday started to explain.

Alexander tried to focus on what Wednesday was suggesting to his mother, but in that moment, China's opinion of him was all that mattered. He blocked out everyone else in the room and his attention zeroed in on China. He walked up to her and asked in a muted tone, "Do you think I did this?"

China scrunched up her face, tilted her head upward slightly to meet his gaze and said, "Are you seriously asking me that question?" She grabbed his left hand. "Of course I don't think you had anything to do with this."

Her words, the spark in her eyes and softened tone had Alexander gifting her with a wide smile. Alexander cupped China's face with his right hand. While he hadn't truly believed that China actually thought he was capable of stealing from his own family's company and endangering the environment, hearing her say those words was like having a set of weights lifted off his heart. Alexander ran the pad of his thumb across China's lips as he gazed into her eyes. In those few short moments, Alexander didn't care about friendship or who might be watching; he needed to taste her.

Alexander took a slight step forward, but then he heard Brice clear his throat and Wednesday say sarcastically, "Now that that's all cleared up…"

Dammit. Alexander dropped his hand and China blinked twice, as if she needed to break their connection before she returned to her seat.

"What do we know?" Brice asked no one in particular.

"We've done an extensive background check on all your employees, including the five people you previously identified, and frankly, only two of them deserve further investigation," Wednesday explained.

"Who?" China asked.

"Ella Higgs, your electronic documents director, and Tom Raddatz, your quality operations director," Wednesday said. The room went still. China opened her mouth to speak, but quickly closed it. She knew just how much Victoria valued her employees, and to think any one of them could betray her, let alone the ones whose careers she'd nurtured over the years, would be heartbreaking.

"They've worked for our company…for me, for several years," Victoria replied, disbelief marring her face.

"I know this is difficult," Wednesday offered, her face expressionless. "But this is why you hired us. We're not emotionally invested in these people. In fact, I found that you have more problems than you realize." Wednesday reached into her bag and pulled out her electronic tablet. "Three additional people had issues in their background that sent up red flags," she shared.

"Such as?" Victoria asked.

Wednesday ran her perfectly manicured nails across her tablet's screen. "Morris Henderson, one of your longshoremen, has a breaking-and-entering conviction on his record, and Sharon Doyle works part-time for the wife of one of your major competitors as a caterer—an Evan Perez Sr. of Perez Energy."

"What?" Victoria's face went blank.

"How'd we miss that?" Brice asked, searching the faces in the room.

"Probably because your HR manager is dirty herself," Wednesday said.

"Terri Thompson? She's been with us for fifteen years," Victoria replied.

"These last few years she's run into financial difficulties," Wednesday explained, reading from her tablet. "She's been sending your new-hire background check and drug test work to a company that's been giving her kickbacks for each referral."

"Dammit!" Alexander pulled out his phone.

China turned in her chair to face Alexander. "Who are you calling?"

"Security, of course. I want her escorted out of the building now," he said, his tone hard.

Wednesday stood. "Alex, wait," she said, earning a sideways look from Victoria.

A corner of China's mouth rose slightly at the daggers

Victoria shot at Wednesday. Greeting Alexander in such an informal and personal way that wasn't family especially in a business setting was something everyone knew Victoria didn't appreciate.

"Let us do our job. We have all these people under surveillance and we're digging deeper into their backgrounds and affiliations. We'll find the guilty parties."

"Fine!" Alexander started pacing the room. "I just can't sit by and do nothing."

China grabbed Alexander's hand on his last pass and looked up at him. "Stop. You're not doing nothing. You have a business to run and revised processes and procedures to put in place. We might not have caused this problem but we have to fix it," China reminded.

Alexander squeezed China's hand before intertwining their fingers. She gave him strength that he wasn't ready to let go of. "You're right. We have to get the system updated and the staff retrained as soon as possible."

Victoria rose slowly and smiled. She wrapped her diamond-clad fingers around the handle of her white bag and said, "I don't care how you all get it done. I just want this problem resolved as soon as possible." Her eyes lasered in on Wednesday. "Move forward with your recommendations," Victoria instructed her. Wednesday nodded her understanding.

"What recommendations?" Alexander questioned.

Victoria checked her watch. "Wednesday will bring everyone up to speed. I have to go. Liz and I are heading out to the park to meet with the caterers about this weekend's picnic. I expect to see everyone there," she said, tossing air kisses as she made her exit.

"Just one moment, Victoria, I'll walk out with you. I have one more recommendation." Wednesday collected her things and left the office.

China pulled her hand free from Alexander. "I should go, too." She gave Alexander and Brice a half smile before she, too, walked out of the office.

Why is she running off so fast? "I better get back to the office." Alexander was starting to follow China when he heard his brother say, "Not so fast, mister."

Damn.

"Close the door. We need to talk," Brice ordered. Alexander complied and turned to face his brother. He recognized that tone, so he knew this conversation wouldn't be about the business.

"All right," he said, folding his arms across his chest. "Let's talk."

Chapter 15

China walked into her office and made a beeline for her desk, where she retrieved a small blue package from one of the drawers. "Thank goodness." She walked over to the mahogany wall-storage system that hung to the left of her desk. She opened a panel door on its base, exposing a hidden refrigerator.

China removed a bottle of water, closed the door and picked up a small crystal glass from one of the shelves. She stood at the side of her desk, poured herself half a glass of water and dropped two tablets from the blue package into the glass. Using her index finger and thumb, China held her nose as she quickly swallowed the fizzy substance. Within seconds, China released a big burp and laughed, turning her head to face her windows. *Brice is right; this bug sure does like me. If I didn't know any better and hadn't had my period, I might actually think I was pregnant. Now, wouldn't that be something?*

"Feel better?" asked an unwelcome but familiar voice.

China sighed, forced a smile and turned to greet her guest. "Wednesday…"

"Looks like you needed that release."

"I did. Can I help you with something?"

"Yes, actually. Got a minute?" Wednesday asked.

"Sure," China reluctantly agreed.

Wednesday closed the door and walked over to one of the chairs that sat in front of China's desk. She placed her Fendi purse on the corner of the desk and her eyes scanned the room. "You have a lovely office. Do all the executive offices have their own private spaces?" She focused on the two closed doors in the corners of the room.

China knew she was referring to Alexander's private lounge area. "We each have a powder room and a mini-walk-in closet. Those were Victoria's ideas when they built the building all those years ago. But only the Kingsleys have three-quarter bathrooms and private space to do whatever they wish."

Wednesday nodded as she walked over to China's shelves. "May I?" she asked before picking up one of the pictures.

"Sure."

It was a photo of China when she was a child, and she was being held by a woman wearing a big hat. "Your mother?" Wednesday asked, holding up the photo for China to see.

"Yes, she loved wearing big hats." China smiled at the memory.

Wednesday returned the picture to its resting place. She gave all the photos and objects the once-over before she leaned forward to give one picture in particular her attention. It was a photo of Alexander and China dressed up and making a toast. She straightened and turned to face China. "Alexander has that same photo in his office."

"I know." China's mouth twisted upward. "Our graduation." Her mind flashed back to the night she and Alexander had celebrated their graduation and passing the bar on the first try with a grand party his mother insisted on throwing. She remembered it as though it were yesterday.

China stood leaning against a baby grand piano in a hallway adjacent to the grand ballroom of the Hilton Americas Houston Hotel. All of their friends were inside enjoying the festivities, but China found herself in the hallway talking to Alexander, trying to compose herself.

"I can't believe your mother did this," she said, shaking her head, looking down at the fifty-thousand-dollar check she'd just been handed by a jubilant Victoria.

"Why not?" Alexander asked, handing her a glass and pouring from the champagne bottle he'd commandeered from one of the wait staff. "It's a gift."

"It's too much."

"Not really. My mother believes in showing gratitude toward people's successes, especially if those accomplishments meet her business needs," he explained, pouring champagne into his own glass.

"In that case, I can only imagine what your check looked like," she said, laughing.

"Oh, no," Alexander said, shaking his head and placing the bottle between them on top of the piano. "Kingsleys don't get gifts for doing well."

China frowned. "What?"

"My mother expects us to do well. Anything less is unacceptable. Graduating at the top of my class and passing the bar the first time is what I'm supposed to do," he said nonchalantly.

China's frown deepened. "So, your mother never celebrated your successes?"

"Always—she just expected them."

"What if you didn't meet them—then what?" she asked.

"That wouldn't happen. When I struggled with math as a kid, my mother hired a math genius to help me until I no longer struggled."

"Wow..."

"It's no big deal. I'm not spoiled but I have had a privileged upbringing and I've never wanted for anything. Well, except maybe a little freedom."

China nodded, taking a drink of her champagne. "Victoria was pretty overprotective when you all were kids, wasn't she?"

"Very, but enough about all that. Let's have an official toast." Alexander topped off their flutes.

"What are we drinking to?" China held up her glass.

"To our friendship." Alexander raised his glass.

"Friends forever..."

"I got it. To us and all of our successes and always having each other's back."

"For life," China added before tapping her glass to his. In that moment, a flash from a roaming photographer captured their private moment and attention.

It was a photo they'd both insisted on keeping.

Wednesday tilted her head slightly. "May I ask you a question?"

Her request brought China back to the present. "Of course."

"When you saw that it was Alexander's login access that was used to manipulate the system, given all that you know about your security, did you...even for a millisecond—" she used her index finger and thumb to illustrate her point "—think that Alexander might have been behind this whole mess?"

China folded her arms across her chest and scowled at Wednesday but remained silent.

"Well?" Wednesday encouraged her.

"Well, I'm trying to determine if this is some kind of test or a really bad joke, because you can't be serious."

"Oh, I am very serious. You're a brilliant woman. You couldn't have possibly just let that go." Wednesday's face contorted. "Unless…"

China could see the speculation on her face. "Unless what?"

"You've known Alexander for, what, seven years now?"

"Correct."

"You claim to be each other's best friends, yet I get the sense there's more to your relationship than either of you are letting on."

"The specific nature of my friendship with Alexander is none of your business, and I don't see how it has anything to do with you or your ridiculous question."

China dropped her hands, moved around her desk and took a seat. Between Wednesday's nonsense question, her headache and her upset stomach, China was afraid she'd get sicker, and she didn't want some kind of physical response to be perceived as agreement with Wednesday's speculation.

A tight smile crawled across Wednesday's face. She ran her hand along the edge of China's desk. "This is a dazzling piece of furniture—a frosted glass top over handcrafted mahogany wood. A gift from Alexander."

"How—"

"How did I know?" Wednesday took a seat. "I know a lot of things."

China raised her eyebrows. "Such as…?"

Wednesday crossed her legs. "You're an army brat who traveled all over the world with your single mother. You graduated at the top of your class at UCLA after attending on a full gymnastic scholarship. You went on to Harvard Law School, which is where you met Alexander. You received several job offers from several prestigious law firms, most of which would have made you partner within five years. You even got an offer from one of my bosses. By the way, that mind trick of yours would've come in handy in our business."

"It's not a trick," she corrected Wednesday.

"Yet you passed on all those opportunities to follow Alexander into his family's company."

China sat forward, intertwined her fingers and set them on her desk. "And what do you think that means?"

"I think you're in love with Alexander in spite of his track record with women. I think you would turn a blind eye to any inappropriate business doings he might undertake."

China frowned. "Do you actually think Alexander is guilty of something?"

"No, I don't. But I think that if he were, you would help him cover it up, which is why you can no longer be a part of this investigation."

"Excuse me…"

"You're too personally involved," Wednesday declared.

"And you're not?" China countered, raising her left eyebrow.

"See, that's the difference between us." Wednesday leaned forward. "I can separate business from pleasure."

"But I—"

Wednesday held up her hand, presumably to stop the protest she knew was coming. "You'll continue handling all the legal aspects of things—writing the responses and so forth, but it will be based off the evidence my team and I bring you. Not on anything that you collect."

"Does Alexander know about this?"

Wednesday tilted her head slightly and smirked. "The fact that you've even asked that question tells me I made the right decision."

"You do work for him," China reminded her.

Wednesday heaved a sigh and rose from her seat. "No, China, I don't work for Alexander. I work for Victoria."

That knocked the wind right out of her sails, because China knew she was right. Victoria was definitely the captain of this ship and she'd always do what was best for her company, including sidelining China herself if she believed it was necessary. There was a knock on China's door.

"I should let you get back to work."

China nodded. "Come in," she called, rising slowly.

Jackson walked in, holding a single red rose and wearing a blue pinstripe suit, white shirt and dress shoes. "How sweet," Wednesday complimented him, a comment China chose to ignore.

"Excuse me, I thought you were alone. Your assistant told me to come right in."

"It's fine. Wednesday Adams, this is—"

"Jackson Weatherly," Wednesday said, offering her hand. "I've heard a lot of great things about you and your practice."

Jackson cut his eyes to China. *Great, now he thinks I've been bragging about him.* China immediately felt guilty for thinking that was even a bad thing. "Wednesday is our investigative consultant. She knows everything about everyone." China knew she should just let him think whatever he wanted, but she just couldn't.

"Pleased to meet you," he replied, shaking her hand

and gifting Wednesday with one of his friendly mega-watt smiles.

"Well, I hope to see you at this weekend's family and friends employee picnic. It should be fun," she shared before walking out the door.

"Family and friends picnic?" Jackson repeated before he kissed China on the cheek and handed her the rose.

"Thank you. It's an annual thing," she said, leaning against her desk.

"You going?"

China knew where he was headed with that question but she wasn't sure she wanted to deal with it. "I haven't decided yet."

Jackson eyed the empty glass and Alka-Seltzer package. "You still not feeling well?" he questioned, frowning.

"I'm fine, just an upset stomach. Why are you all dressed up?"

"I had a meeting downtown and I thought I would try and convince you to have lunch with me."

"That's sweet, but I really do have a great deal to get done in a short amount of time. Joyce is going to run out and pick us up something to eat in a little while."

Jackson took both her hands into his. He stared down at her. "You would tell me if you decided this wasn't working for you after all, wouldn't you?" he asked.

"Yes, of course."

Jackson pulled her into a big hug. He released her and leaned in for a kiss. China could see the desire in his eyes. She knew Jackson expected to receive that long-awaited, passionate type of kiss they'd yet to experience. The type of kiss she hadn't been able to share since kissing and making love to Alexander. Before China had to reject Jackson again, there was another knock on her door. "Come in," she quickly called. *Please.*

Jackson pushed out an audible breath, his frustration clear. He released China's hands and stepped away from her. "Excuse me, China. Ben took your car for service and Alexander left this for you." Joyce handed her a key fob.

China nodded her head. "Thanks."

Joyce walked out, closing the door behind her. "What's the key for?" Jackson asked.

"It's the key to Alexander's car. I use his whenever mine gets serviced."

"That's…nice of him. I guess."

"It's no big deal," she said. "The company services all the executives' vehicles."

"Do you all switch cars, too?" His jaw clenched.

China knew Jackson's obvious annoyance was justified. She also knew she needed to make a decision about where things were really going between them, but now wasn't the time. "So, you busy Saturday?"

"Saturday?"

"The company picnic, remember? Care to be my date?"

Chapter 16

Brice moved to stand behind his vertical desk. Alexander came farther into the room, leaned against the stationary desk with his right hand in his pocket. "What's up?"

"What's the deal with you and China?"

"Not this again." He checked his watch. "I have a meeting soon, but I took your advice. I'm staying in the friend zone, giving her just what she wants."

"It didn't look that way ten minutes ago when you groped her in front of everyone."

"I did no such thing," Alexander protested.

"You might as well have." Brice gave his brother the side eye.

"Look, I told you, I'm being supportive. I'm even being supportive of her relationship with what's-his-name." His expression hardened.

"You mean her *friendship* with what's-his-name," Brice corrected.

"What?"

"They're just friends. They're getting to know each other." He raised his hands as if to surrender. "Her words, not mine."

Alexander gave Brice a half smile. "Just friends," he echoed. Alexander thought back to the night they'd crossed that friendship line, and the idea of China doing the same with Jackson set his mouth in a hard line.

"That was a quick transition." Brice laughed. "I bet I can guess what you were just thinking, too."

Alexander ran both hands down his face. "Are you going to stand there and give me crap, or do you have more sage advice for me?"

"Depends." The corners of Brice's mouth quirked up.

Alexander's eyebrows rose. "On what?"

"Have you figured out what you want yet?"

Alexander pushed out a quick breath, walked over to the window and pulled out his cell phone. He flipped through his pictures until he found the one he was looking for. It was a picture of him and China at last year's picnic, and they held the blue ribbon they'd received after winning the dance-off. He held up his phone for Brice to see. "Remember this?"

Brice came from around his desk, stood next to Alexander and studied the picture. "Sure. You two danced your butts off for that tiny ribbon. Talk about competitive."

"Do you remember what happened after that weekend?" His expression dulled.

Brice gave his head a slow shake. "I have no idea."

"I spent the next three weeks working with Morgan on the rigs in the Gulf."

Recognition blossomed over Brice's face. "I do remember that. Mom was pissed. She never understood why you felt the need to escape from the office for so long. Frankly, neither did I."

"This is why." Alexander held up the photo again.

"I don't get it. You look happy. In fact, you look happier than I've ever seen you, before or since, really."

"I left because that's when I knew," he said, staring down at the picture. "*This* is what I want. I left because I figured out that I was having romantic feelings for China and I knew her only focus at the time was growing her career. I had to pull it together for the sake of our friendship."

"So you ran," Brice murmured.

Alexander nodded. "I ran. I had to go find a way to put the genie back in the bottle. I'll admit the company of a few ladies helped to take the sting out of my realization. All's well that ends well, right?" He put his phone away and walked over to the freestanding bar that been placed on the left side of the room. "Want one?"

"Hell, it's five somewhere. Get the Hennessy Pure White at the bottom of the cabinet."

Alexander pulled out the bottle and poured two fingers into each glass. He handed one to his brother, held his up and said, "To regrets."

Alexander tossed back the smooth liquid, hoping the sting of the cognac would calm the raging emotions threatening to take control. He followed that one with another before putting the glass on the bar and taking a seat on the sofa next to it.

Brice finished off his drink, put the glass down and stood over his brother. "What if you were wrong?"

"What are you talking about?" Alexander was leaning forward, rubbing his hands together.

"What if she loved you, too, then and now?" Brice sat next to his brother. "You two have always had a special bond that skirted the edges of something more. I think you both were just too scared to do anything about it."

"And now?" Alexander wondered out loud.

"Well, that's up to you, big brother." He slapped Alexander's back and returned to his desk. "What about the kid thing?"

"I want them…eventually, but the idea of me and kids scares me to death."

"Why?" Brice asked frowning.

"The idea of leaving one here, especially a boy…my son, to fight this world alone without being properly prepared by his father makes my head hurt."

"Like the way we had to grow up without a dad," Brice agreed, nodding.

"Yes. That doesn't make you think twice when it comes to having children?"

"Well, I'd have to get a wife again, first," Brice teased.

"Seriously, man, how do you feel about having kids?"

"I want them. In fact, I might have them with or without a wife."

"Now you sound like China." Alexander sat back in the sofa. "Although, it doesn't seem like such a scary idea when I think about having them with China."

"There you go. Now all you have to do is win her over from homeboy—and telling her how you feel won't be enough, since she knows you too well. She'll just think she's only a challenge for you. You have to show her how sincere you really are. Think you can do that?"

"I'm a Kingsley." Alexander laid his head back, put his feet up on the coffee table and closed his eyes.

"Yeah, one with his own office, too," Brice reminded Alexander as he adjusted his computer screen.

"I need forty-five minutes to formulate my strategy."

"And sleep off that buzz," Brice observed.

Alexander laughed. "That, too."

Joyce walked into China's office. "You and Mr. GQ have plans for lunch?"

China looked up from the document she was editing. "No. If I'm lucky, I won't have to see him until the picnic."

"If you're lucky?" Joyce's brows came together.

China could see confusion marring Joyce's face. "I need time and space to get my head together."

"So, you're taking him to the picnic?" Joyce asked, frowning.

"Looks like it." China folded her arms on her desk and dropped her head.

"What's the deal? That man is dangerously sexy and worth all the time I'd get for performing numerous illegal acts with him."

China's head popped up. "Joyce," she said, laughing.

"What? The man's fine as hell, and according to you, very sweet. Wait…that's it, isn't it?" Joyce shook her head and took a seat.

"I have no idea what you're talking about," China said.

"You want a bad boy. I understand, but they start to wear on you real quick, trust me."

"Why are you in my office?" China picked up her pen and resumed editing her document.

"Just checking on you. What are you working on?" Joyce asked.

"Our ninety-day response. I'm going over all the details to make sure we haven't missed anything."

"Speaking of missing stuff…"

China looked up. "What?"

"I got tea to spill about our little mystery. I'm not sure how true this is—after all, it is gossip."

"You never know, so spit it out." China put her pen down and gave Joyce her undivided attention. At this point, she'd take all the information she could get; she wanted to find answers.

Joyce scooted her chair closer to the desk, looked over her shoulder as if she wanted to make sure no one was standing behind her and leaned forward. China copied Joyce's move. She just hoped all the cloak-and-dagger stuff was worth it. "What is it, already?"

"Sharon Doyle works part-time for Evan Perez Senior." Her eyebrows danced and she added, "At night…"

China sat back in her chair as her sense of hope disappeared. "We know that already. She does catering for his wife."

"Yeah." Joyce folded her arms, crossed her legs and pursed her lips. "If his wife doesn't mind her catering to her husband's needs—his very specific and nasty needs."

China's eyes grew wide as saucers. "What?"

"Yes. Rumor has it she started off working for his wife but quickly became his personal assistant on a part-time basis, nights only."

"He's old enough to be her daddy."

"Yeah, her sugar daddy." Joyce snapped two fingers in the air.

"As gross and wrong as that may be, I'm not sure how this information can help us find out who's trying to sabotage our company. Besides—" China took a sip out of her water bottle "—I've been ordered off the investigation. It seems I'm too personally involved."

"So what? That makes you even more motivated to find the truth. Whose bright idea was that?"

"Victoria put Wednesday in charge, so for now, what Wednesday says goes. Anyway, this is all rumor, and there may not be anything to any of this."

"But there can also be some truth in it, too, and there's only one way to find out," Joyce said, offering her friend and boss a mischievous grin.

"What are you talking about?"

"Pam Gray, who works in the mailroom, was friends with Sharon. They used to hang out. They even went to the same hair salon until they had some kind of blowup. Anyway, Pam's stylist's baby daddy's sister overheard Sharon talking on the phone in the salon one day. She heard her saying that she was tired of being Evan's personal dictation machine."

"Wait, what?" China burst out laughing, bringing her hands to her mouth.

"Listen," Joyce said excitedly, waving her hands. "It gets better. She said that meeting him at ZaZa's every night was getting old, and if he didn't show her that he was serious about being with her, he could find someone else to do his dirty work."

"Girl, shut up." China couldn't stop laughing. It was the first time in a long time that she actually felt like her old self. With everything that was going on with the company, her health issues and her emotions bouncing all over the place, she could use a good reason to laugh.

"Everyone knows how much Evan Perez hates Victoria, especially after she beat him and his company out of several major contracts," Joyce reminded.

"And your point is?"

"My point is, he would do anything to bring this company down and if he has to use some young chick to do it—" she shook her head "—you know he would."

China nodded. "And what better way to do that than to sic the EPA on us?"

Joyce clapped. "I have a great idea."

China's eyes narrowed. She could almost see the lightbulb going off in her friend's brain. "Why am I suddenly so afraid?"

"I have no clue, especially since all of my ideas are usually quite brilliant," Joyce bragged. "Let's go have a drink tonight at ZaZa's."

"Oh, no," China said, shaking her hands and head.

"Why not? I hear they have a great happy hour and dinner buffet from six to ten. It's just two friends having dinner and drinks after work. If we happen to see something…"

"Like, what, two people meeting? We don't even know what time they meet. Besides, how would that help our case, Nancy Drew?"

"Your employee, one with the right type of access, I might add, is having an affair with one of your biggest competitors. How is that alone not suspicious? Anyway, Pam's stylist's baby daddy's sister got Sharon talking because she knew she wanted to vent, and before she knew it, she told her that they met at nine o'clock on the dot. It seems he's timely with everything he does."

"TMI. I guess we could tell Wednesday what we suspect and let her handle it."

"And let her take all the credit?" Joyce rolled her eyes. "Hell, no."

China sighed. "This is crazy."

Joyce started bouncing in her seat, rubbing her hands together. "What time do we leave?"

Chapter 17

China and Joyce walked through the lobby of the ZaZa Hotel, a premier Houston establishment located in the museum district. China was surprised by the unique contemporary furnishings that greeted their entrance. "Wow, this is different," she said, eyeing the large animal-print chairs scattered throughout the lobby.

"Cool, right?" Joyce said.

They passed an oval wooden desk with a mirror front, where a tall, handsome man greeted them with a wide smile. Joyce returned his smile with a half wave as they made their way to the elevator. "The lounge is on the second floor," Joyce informed China.

"Do you know him, and how do you know where the lounge is? I thought you said you'd never been here before," China questioned.

"I know a lot of people, and I said I've never been to the happy hour or buffet before," Joyce replied with a wink.

The elevator doors opened. China entered the car, saying, "I can't believe I let you talk me into this. I feel like we should be wearing dark sunglasses and trench coats."

Joyce hit the number two button. "Chill. Remember why we're here—to clear our company's name, not to mention Alexander's. This will be fun, and you need a night out. By the way, you feeling okay?"

"Physically, yes, but mentally...the jury's still out," China said.

Joyce laughed. The doors opened to a gorgeous room full of well-dressed professionals, many of whom China recognized. They exited the elevator and walked past a mirrored wall with several food stations lined up in front of it. To their right, two six-foot-long bars had been set up and were staffed by some of the most good-looking people she'd ever seen. Joyce led their way through the crowd of mingling people and past various tables centered around a large wooden dance floor.

"Why would anyone have a clandestine meeting in such a public place?"

"Like the old saying goes, hide in plain sight. There." Joyce pointed at an empty, four-seat table in the corner of the room. "It's perfect. We can see the whole room."

"Yes, and they can see us, too." As if on cue, she heard her name being called. She turned to see a tall blonde dressed in a yellow-and-black suit waving as she approached.

"Hi," China replied, searching her mind, but for the life of her, she couldn't remember how or if she knew this woman. She cut her eyes to Joyce, who offered her a small shrug.

"You don't remember me, do you?" The woman frowned.

"I'm sorry, but I don't," China replied.

"It's okay. We met at a seminar on torts a few years ago. I'm Claire Star." Her face shone with excitement as she introduced herself.

"Nice to meet you," China said.

"Please excuse my manners," she said to Joyce, placing her hands over her chest in a dramatic fashion. "I'm Claire Star."

"Hi, I'm Joyce." She gave a two-finger wave. "If you'll excuse me, I'm going to go catch that table before we lose it."

China glared at Joyce as she disappeared through the crowd. "I won't keep you," Claire promised. "I was hoping I could get you to do me a favor."

"Which is?"

"You still work for Kingsley Oil and Gas, right?" Claire reached into her purse, pulled out one of her business cards and handed it to her.

"Yes…"

"Great gig, by the way. Alexander is an amazing man, and I know he only dates beautiful and successful women. Since I easily meet his criteria, I was hoping you could pass my card on to him and put in a good word for me." She batted her eyes. "I know you two are good friends."

China stared down at the card. *Are we in high school?* She felt a wave of anger and a sense of possessiveness toward Alexander that she'd never felt before. China fought to maintain control to no avail. Her left hand rose and landed on her hip. She opened her mouth to simply deny the other woman's requests when all manner of crazy came flying out. "Are you kidding me? What do you think you'll get from Alexander, other than a hookup? It certainly won't be marriage, because that's the last thing on his mind. Oh, wait, maybe not the last thing—that would be having kids." China noticed that she had gained the attention of a few partygoers.

"On second thought," Claire said, taking back her card, "I'll take care of it myself."

Claire walked away and China quickly dropped her hand, smiling at a few onlookers. "What the hell's wrong with you?" she whispered to herself. *You know what's wrong and it's time you dealt with it.* China wove her way around the patrons over to the table that Joyce seized and sat with her back to the crowd.

Joyce was sitting in front of several plates of finger foods. "What was that all about? It looked intense," Joyce asked, bringing a glass of white wine to her lips with one hand while using her other to slide the glass of red to China.

"Nothing," China replied before taking a sip of the wine. She put the glass down and shivered. "That tastes funny."

"Really?" Joyce reached for the glass and took a sip. "Taste fine to me. You want to order something else?"

"No, this is fine." China picked up the glass of water that sat closest to her and started drinking it. She was hoping it would drown the rage that suddenly and so unexpectedly flared inside of her.

"So?" Joyce inquired.

"So what?"

"What did the blonde goddess want?" Joyce took a bite out of one of her sliders.

China shook her head and sat back in her chair. "She wanted me to pass her card on to Alexander and put in a good word for her."

Joyce's head fell forward and she laughed. "What? Booty call by proxy. Some people, just ridiculous."

China sat with her hands in her lap. "I guess."

"Is it in your purse?" Joyce asked excitedly. "Let's prank call her."

"What?" China frowned.

"The card, let me see it," Joyce requested before taking another bite of her food.

China dropped her eyes, feeling completely embarrassed by her behavior. "She took it back."

"Why? And why aren't you eating anything? The food here is great."

"I'm not hungry."

"Why would she give it to you, just to take it back?" Joyce asked, looking past China's shoulders, waving and smiling at passersby.

China looked up at her friend and said, "I basically told her she would be wasting her time unless all she wanted was a simple hookup."

Joyce laughed. "I guess she didn't appreciate your advice."

"I guess not."

"That's my song," Joyce said, wiping her mouth. "Let's go dance."

China glanced over at the crowded dance floor. "Line dancing isn't dancing, not really. It's more like follow the leader."

"Really?"

"Yes, really. Dancing should be intimate, regardless of the tempo of the music." China smiled as she thought back to when she danced with Alexander at last year's picnic.

"Well, whatever it is, I love it." Joyce waved her hands in the air.

"Let's get out of here." China reached for her purse and pulled out her phone. "We've been here an hour too long already."

"Nope," Joyce said, shaking her head and swaying to the music. "It's still early and we've got a job to do."

China noticed she'd missed two calls from Wednesday and rolled her eyes skyward.

"What's up?"

"Wednesday called me. I wonder what she wants." China returned her phone to her purse.

Joyce looked up and the joyfulness of her demeanor and the wide smile on her face disappeared. "I think you're about to find out," she said, looking over China's shoulder.

China's forehead creased. "What are you talking about?"

Her answer came in the form of her name being called from behind. "China, girl, is that you?" a voice with a deep Southern accent said.

China turned in her chair to see Wednesday headed her way, wearing a pair of tight jeans, a multicolored blouse and stilettos, and carrying two shot glasses. Walking at her side was an attractive, brown-skinned woman wearing a similar outfit, only her blouse was red. She, too, was carrying a pair of shot glasses. *What's with the fake accent?* "Time to get this party started, ladies," Wednesday all but shouted, taking the seat next to China. "Sit down, Jolly-girl. Tequila shots for all."

"What you doing here, Wednesday?" China said.

"That's a damn good question. I'm working. Why don't you tell us exactly what *you're* doing here?" she said, her voice barely above a whisper.

"Us?" China looked over at the woman Wednesday called Jolly who was now sitting to her right.

Wednesday picked up her shot glass. "Toast time," she yelled out, excitedly garnering the attention of a few folks at nearby tables. "Pick up your glasses, ladies," she ordered through gritted teeth.

Joyce complied but China said, "I'm not much of a te-quila drinker."

"Then this should suit your delicate constitution just fine. Pick up the glass, China." A wide smile crawled across Wednesday's face but her tone was harsh.

China raised her glass.

"To a great night," Jolly said.

The other three ladies tossed their tequila back first. China braced herself for the sting of the taste and followed suit, only it never came—the glasses held unsweetened tea. Wednesday and Jolly slammed theirs down and started clapping, cheering and bouncing in their chairs.

"Just go with it." Jolly smiled and whispered to a confused-looking Joyce.

Joyce reached for a glass of water as though she needed a chaser. "That was…different."

"What type of game are you two playing?" China glared at Wednesday.

"That's just it. This isn't the game that you and Louise over there seem to think it is."

"Louise?" Joyce grimaced.

Wednesday and Jolly turned and stared at Joyce. China sighed and tilted her head slightly. "The movie *Thelma and Louise*…"

"Oh, I love that movie, hated the ending," Joyce said.

"Jolly and I have a job to do, and we can't do it if we have to watch out for you, too."

China sat forward slightly. "Wait, you know about Sharon Doyle and Evan Perez?"

"Of course we do, which is why we're here. What I don't understand is why *you're* here, especially since I ordered you to stand down."

"Ordered…" Joyce said, her eyebrows standing at attention.

China held up her left hand, stopping Joyce from making a scene. "We didn't think you knew about them, since everything we know was based on rumors and innuendo."

"You'd be surprised how much truth can be found in rumors and innuendo."

"Told you," Joyce declared proudly.

"Now what?" China asked, feeling foolish.

"Now it's time for you two to get out of here before Sharon and Evan show up. There's a limo waiting outside for you," Wednesday explained to China.

"Oh, I came with Joyce, she'll take me home."

Joyce nodded as she wrapped the last two sliders in a paper napkin, placing them in her purse. Wednesday's brows snapped together at her actions. "Sorry, you don't have a choice in the matter."

China sighed because she knew that could only mean one thing. "I'll see you tomorrow, Joyce."

"That's cool, but, Wednesday, I gotta know something."

"And what might that be, Joyce?" Wednesday was clearly annoyed by their antics.

"What was up with that unsweetened tea masquerading as tequila?"

Wednesday smirked. "We never drink while working."

"That sucks," Joyce said as she, China and Wednesday made their way to the elevator.

"I'll walk you out," Wednesday said.

After exiting onto the ground level, Joyce headed out of the front door while China took a side exit, Wednesday on her heels. She walked through a sliding glass door where she was greeted by a driver.

"Ms. Edwards?"

"Yes." China looked back to see a giddy Wednesday waving goodbye.

"Ready?" the driver asked.

"Might as well be." The driver opened the door and China leaned forward, looked into the car and said, "Good evening, Victoria."

Chapter 18

"Get in, China," Victoria ordered, patting the seat.

China slid into the car and sat with her legs crossed at the ankles. She felt as if she was waiting to be scolded by her school principal. The tense-looking Victoria wore a long, black, sleeveless gown that sparkled like the stars in the sky. A diamond cuff bracelet decorated the wrist of her left hand, which held a glass of champagne.

"Care for a glass, dear?" she asked, but didn't budge to accommodate her unenthusiastic guest. It was a familiar ploy that told China the offer was superficial and this wouldn't be a warm and fuzzy conversation.

"No, thank you," China replied.

Victoria pushed a button to raise the partition, signaling the driver that she was ready to leave. After riding in silence for nearly ten minutes, Victoria finally asked, "Do you remember when you were in law school and Alexander brought you to Houston to meet me?"

"How could I forget?" China's thoughts flashed back to the day that changed her career trajectory.

"Alexander, are you sure about this?" China asked, resting her napkin across her lap.

"Of course I am. We have a position open that you're perfect for, and you need a job for the summer." Alexander picked up the menu and started reading it.

"That's not what I'm talking about."

"Then what are *you talking about?" he asked, looking up from his menu.*

"I'm talking about my moving into your apartment. How's your mother going to feel about it?"

Alexander placed his menu to the side. "The key in that sentence is that it's my *apartment. Anyway, she's not like that. Besides, you're moving into my place...not in with me."*

"She may not see the difference."

"Sure she will. I won't be there, and she knows I don't like leaving my apartment empty while I'm working offshore," he explained.

"I don't know." She shook her head.

"I guess we're about to find out." China and Alexander watched as his mother approached. Her hair was pulled back into a tight bun and she wore a rust-colored pantsuit; she stopped to speak to several other patrons as she made her way over to Alexander. He stood and greeted his mother with a kiss on both cheeks before turning his attention back to his guest. "Victoria Kingsley, this is China Edwards," Alexander introduced them.

China rose, presented her hand and offered up a tentative smile. While Victoria was strikingly beautiful, China couldn't get over how young she looked. Her smooth, wrinkle-free skin made it hard to believe that this woman was old enough to have grown children. It wasn't some-thing she was used to. "I'm very pleased to meet you, Mrs. Kingsley."

Victoria shook her hand and smiled. "Please, call me Victoria."

They all took a seat and were immediately approached by an eager-looking waiter. "Would you like your usual, Ms. Victoria?"

"Yes, Scott, thank you," she confirmed, turning to Alexander and China. "You two ready to order?"

"I am but China may need—"

"I'm ready."

After all the orders had been placed, Victoria trained her eyes on China. "My son tells me you're extremely qualified for my legal research assistant position. You do realize this is temporary, but a full-time position for the summer?"

"Yes, ma'am."

Victoria turned to her son. "And did you explain to China my definition of full-time, Alexander?"

"No, I was hoping you would be a little more reason-able now that you're getting older. After all, you just had a birthday."

Victoria smiled and said, "I haven't." She turned to face a concerned-looking China. "Let me be clear about my expectations. As a well-paid employee, you are expected to give one hundred and fifty percent every day and be available to work when needed, which is usually ten- to twelve-hour days, including weekends when necessary. Do you have a problem with that?"

"No, ma'am."

"Mother doesn't think we need lives outside of work," Alexander replied sarcastically.

Victoria gave Alexander the side eye. "Don't listen to

my ridiculous son, China. I want my family, as well as anyone who works for me, to have an excellent life." She turned and glared at her son. *"I just think you should work hard so that you can pay for it."*

"I have no problem with the hours, Mrs. Kingsley," China assured the woman with what she hoped was a confident smile.

"Good, and for the last time, it's Victoria." She took a drink from her water glass. *"As for living in my son's apartment—"*

"I understand if you have some reservations with those arrangements, but I assure you that the only thing between me and Alexander is friendship," she explained nervously.

Victoria sighed. She leaned forward and placed her hand over China's. *"Relax. I don't care who my son sleeps with, because he knows better than to bring any type of mess and drama into my company. If I thought for a second that you would be a problem for any reason, I wouldn't hire you."* China glanced over at Alexander, who simply shrugged and nodded. *"In fact, I think we'll be good friends. But understand this—"*

"Here we go," Alexander interrupted, rolling his eyes, an action Victoria ignored.

"No matter how close we may become, if you become a problem for me or my business, you'll be gone faster than you can catch a breath."

Alexander reached over and patted China on the shoulder. *"Don't feel bad. She gave me, my brothers and my cousins that same speech. Mother's all about her business."*

"That I am, and don't you ever forget it, Mister Heir Apparent." She pulled back her hand and gestured for the waiter to come forward.

China hadn't noticed that the staff had been waiting for

Victoria's signal before approaching the table. The waiter placed their first course in front of them. "Let's enjoy our lunch, shall we?"

"Alexander told you then, China, that I was all about my business. A fact you've witnessed firsthand over the years, have you not?"

"I have," she confirmed.

"Then why would you defy an order of mine, regardless of who was issuing it?" Victoria took a sip of her champagne.

China knew she was referring to her issues with Wednesday. "I just wanted to help find whoever is behind all this," she murmured, looking down at her fidgeting hand.

"I understand that, but I'm paying a stellar organization to do that for us and I need for you to stop interfering. Am I making myself clear?" Victoria asked, her face expressionless.

"Yes, of course." China held Victoria's gaze.

"Good. Is there anything else you'd like to get off your chest? You know that you're like a daughter to me and I'm here if you need to talk."

"I do and I'm fine. Thank you for asking," she said.

"All right, then. Now that I've had to cut my evening short, you're stuck with me. We're going to dinner, then I'll drop you off at home." Victoria finished the last of her champagne and put her glass in the holder. She opened her purse, pulled out the key fob that had been sitting on China's desk and handed it to her. "Here you go. I had Alexander's car brought to your house."

China smiled. "You think of everything, Victoria."

"Don't you forget that, either." Both women laughed.

* * *

Alexander rang the doorbell of the penthouse suite in one of Houston's largest downtown apartment buildings. The door opened, and a slightly taller and younger version of himself appeared, wearing a black monogrammed towel wrapped around his waist. "I'm not interrupting anything, am I?" Alexander asked.

"Not now," KJ said, laughing and bumping fists with his brother. "Come in."

"Thanks."

"What's up? Your phone message was cryptic as hell."

"Sorry about this. I know you have to hit the road in the morning, so I won't keep you long."

"It's cool. Let me go change real quick." KJ walked around his sunken living room and disappeared into the back of the apartment while Alexander made his way over to the bar in the corner next to the door. He opened the minirefrigerator and pulled out a beer.

A clothed KJ reappeared, coming from the kitchen carrying a glass with a green substance in it. "Okay, what's going on?" he asked, walking down a second set of steps and sitting on the sofa across from his brother.

"Seriously, man, why did you build a sunken living room in the middle of your apartment?" Alexander asked with a deep scowl. "And what the hell are you drinking?"

"I didn't. The penthouse came with an indoor pool in the middle of the room and I didn't want one, so I had to do something different." KJ held up his glass. "This, my dear brother, is an energy drink that I use to build up my stamina. But you didn't come over here to talk about my dietary habits or my decorating skills."

"No, I didn't." Alexander finished off his beer. "I need some advice about my love life, or lack of one right now."

KJ raised both eyebrows. "From the world's biggest player—isn't that what you and Brice always call me?"

"And I wonder why we call you that, Mister I've Got a Woman in Every Town My Team Travels To."

"Not every town," KJ clarified, laughing. "So what gives?"

Alexander sat back and spent the next thirty minutes bringing his brother up to speed on how his relationship with China had changed. "So…what? You need me to tell you how to win China back?"

"Basically…hell, I don't know what I need. No offense to Brice, but we both know his current situation, and Morgan is as big of a confirmed bachelor as you are."

KJ took another drink from his glass. "What makes you think I know what you should do? I'm not exactly the permanent relationship type, either."

"Yes, but you have a close relationship with China. For some reason, she thinks she needs to play a protective big-sister role with you. I never understood it, but whatever."

KJ smirked. "You can blame that on Mom. Having never had a daughter of her own—and add the fact that China's brilliant—she found the perfect surrogate. Mom made your then-twenty-one-year-old best friend part of this family seven years ago. Her ability to understand grief in such a profound way with the loss of her own mother—well, she was a natural fit with our clan. Plus, China liked being seen as a big sister to all of us—except you, of course."

"What do you mean?"

"Besides the fact that you were the oldest, China always looked at you differently than the rest of us," KJ informed his brother, smirking.

Alexander's face brightened. "Really? You think so?"

"So do you." KJ sat forward with his forearms resting on his knees. "Let me ask you something. Why now?"

"I'm tired of fighting it. I can't go another moment without making her mine...permanently."

"So, I assume you haven't told China that you're in love with her? You do love her, right?"

Alexander met his brother's gaze. "So damn much I...I can't..." He lowered his head and shook it slowly.

"Can't what? You've never been at a loss for words before."

Alexander ran his right hand through his hair before resting it against the back of his neck. "Man, she's my strength. The idea of China turning to someone else, being with them...loving them..."

Alexander began to feel hot, and it was like all the oxygen had suddenly disappeared from the room. He dropped his hand and jumped up. Then he quickly climbed the few steps and walked out onto KJ's terrace, where he gripped the iron railing and tightened his muscles in order to stay upright. He inhaled a couple of deep breaths, trying to pull as much air into his lungs as he could.

KJ followed his brother outside and watched with real concern in his eyes as Alexander tried to bring himself back under control. It was rare that Alexander allowed anyone to see his emotions overtake him in such a way.

"You good?" KJ asked.

"Yeah..."

"*Soooo*, I take that as a no. You haven't told her yet?"

Alexander stood and relaxed his muscles. "I plan to. I just have to figure out how."

"You will. This is China we're talking about. You know her better than anyone, and I'm willing to bet your feelings will be reciprocated."

Alexander turned and faced his brother. "What if you're wrong?"

"I'm not," KJ said confidently.

Alexander rubbed his chin with the knuckles of his right hand.

"Do it soon, A, because that little—" he waved his hand in front of his brother "—whatever it was, isn't a good look."

Alexander gave him a lopsided grin. "I agree, and I think I may have just figured out what to do."

Chapter 19

China stood next to the black Aston Martin that she'd just exited, fishing through her purse for her Ray-Bans. When she found them and retrieved the sunglasses from their case, she placed them over her eyes, shielding them from the sting of the sun. China folded her arms and stared at Joyce, who was taking her time about leaving the luxury vehicle.

"Girl, that's one smooth ride," she declared, adjusting the red romper she wore and pulling her sunglasses down from her head.

"Stop fidgeting with your clothes. You look fine," China said, clicking the car's alarm. "Let's go."

"Don't hate because you have to wear the company's uniform and can't style out like yours truly." Joyce laughed.

China looked down at her blue-jean shorts and white V-neck shirt with the company's name and logo placed over her left breast. "I like what I'm wearing, thank you very much."

"What's the hurry? It's barely four and this goes until ten."

China waved. "I just don't want to be late."

Both women headed down a graveled walkway, a path that led them up a small hill toward three tents, two large and one small. Joyce was complaining about the small pieces of gravel getting in her sandals, while China gloated about being smart enough to wear tennis shoes.

"We've all been under a lot of stress. Today's supposed to be fun, so try and enjoy yourself," Joyce encouraged China.

"That's the plan."

"Good. Now, when do you get your car back? Because if I were you, I'd hold off as long as possible. Alexander's is the bomb."

"Ben says it's ready now. When we leave here, we'll swing by the office so I can pick it up," China informed her.

"Yeah, about that…"

"What?" China asked, her eyes narrowed.

"I'm planning to catch a ride back with Lester." Joyce's face and eyes sparkled with joy.

"What, Lester is back?" China loved how her friend's face lit up every time she mentioned her on-again, off-again crush.

Joyce nodded like a bobblehead doll. "All the offshore teams got back late last night. He'll be here sometime later this evening."

"So, you think you two can make it work this time?"

"We can always make it work." Joyce laughed as she nudged her friend.

"You know what I'm saying." China returned her friend's nudge.

"Yeah, but not all of us are looking for a long-term commitment."

"You sound like Alexander," China murmured, her eyes lowered as her heart ached for the man she shouldn't want.

"I'm just trying to enjoy whatever time we have together. Dating an offshore man isn't easy. Speaking of not easy, I thought Jackson was coming."

"He is. He just has to spend a few hours at the hospital first," China explained.

"You better hurry up and deal with it," Joyce declared.

"Deal with what?" China feigned ignorance.

"Whatever it is that's holding you back from being with that good-looking man."

China knew Joyce was right. She had to come to terms and deal with her feelings for Jackson and Alexander, regardless of the consequences.

Joyce stopped and marveled at the sight before them. China smiled without even looking up. The Kingsleys were known for their extravagant parties and events, and by the look of things, today wouldn't be any different.

"You okay?" China asked Joyce, laughing.

"Are you seeing what I'm seeing?" Joyce adjusted her sunglasses as if they were reflecting a faulty image.

"If you're seeing a tent filled with game machines, multiple mounted television sets, and pool and foosball tables, then yes, I'm seeing what you're seeing."

"So that tent—" Joyce pointed to the left side of the field "—with a large chandelier hovering above a huge, wooden dance floor and food stations, is real, too?"

China threw her head back and laughed. "Yes, that's real, too, and so are the portable AC units in both tents."

"Those tents the size of football fields."

"Not quite, but close enough," China said.

"Tammy, where are you going?" Joyce asked the approaching woman holding two plates covered in foil. "The picnic's behind you."

Tammy laughed. "I know, but Sam just got called into work, so he's dropping me off at home before going in."

"You don't have to leave. I'll take you home," China offered.

"I'm not much in a party mood, anyway. It's been a long week and we have an even longer one next week, with those computer experts coming in to do another security sweep."

"Well, you have a good evening," China said.

"Bye, girl." Joyce waved.

"You, too," Tammy replied as she walked toward the parking lot.

"What computer sweep is she talking about?" Joyce asked.

"I have no idea. I'm sure it's something Wednesday set up," China speculated.

"Damn, girl, these Kingsleys are something else," Joyce complimented the family, taking in the sights before her.

"Yes, they are." *Especially Alexander.* "Now let's go find a table."

"What's up, bro?" Brice walked up to Alexander, who was standing at a bar where an old-fashioned soda fountain had been set up.

"Same old, same old. You good?"

"Yep." Brice scanned the tents. "Looks like Mom and Auntie stepped up their game with this year's picnic."

"Did you doubt that they would?" Alexander asked before finishing off his soda.

"Not at all." Brice nodded his head in China's direction. "I see your girl's here."

"Of course she's here. It's an employee and family event. China is basically both."

"That she is. So, when do you plan to make that official?"

Before Alexander could answer, his mother approached the microphone in the DJ booth. "Good afternoon, everyone," Victoria said, smiling as she looked around the tent. "Welcome to this year's Kingsley Annual Picnic."

Victoria spent the next twenty minutes thanking everyone for their service and going over the list of activities available to enjoy, as well as the evening's schedule. Alexander spent the entire time staring at China. He'd always thought she was most striking when she wore little to no makeup, had her hair pulled back into a high ponytail and showed off her athletic body in shorts, and today was no exception. Victoria ended her speech to roaring applause and a standing ovation.

Alexander and China's eyes met and his body came to life. China's smile was like a gift and a magnet that drew him toward her. "Excuse me, Brice." Alexander held her gaze as he moved through the crowd. Unfortunately Jackson's sudden appearance halted him in his tracks. "Dammit…" His smile slipped.

"What's wrong, Alexander?" Wednesday asked, coming up behind him.

He turned and faced her. "Nothing's wrong. When did you get here?"

"A few minutes ago. We still good?"

"Of course. Why do you ask?" His eyebrows snapped together.

"Oh, I don't know. Maybe because you look like your head is about to shoot off like a rocket."

Alexander ran his left hand down his face. "I'm cool."

"Good, because all of our suspects are where they need to be, and if things go as planned, we'll know who's behind all of this by the end of the night."

"I hope so. I still can't believe—"

"There you are," Victoria said, approaching Alexander with her arms extended.

"Mother," he replied, stepping into her embrace.

"Nephew," his aunt Elizabeth said, moving in for a hug of her own.

"Well, well, matching blue-jean skirts—that's different and pretty cute," he complimented them, smiling.

"Liz insisted that we coordinate this year," Victoria explained, rolling her eyes and shaking her head.

"Well, you two ladies did it again. Another great Kingsley event."

Elizabeth clapped her hands. "I know, right?"

"Modest, too," he teased.

"Wednesday, my dear, have you had a chance to take care of that matter we discussed this morning?"

"Not yet, Victoria, but I will."

"Be sure that you do…today," Victoria ordered.

"Yes, ma'am."

"Come, Elizabeth, let's go find the rest of our children."

Alexander watched as his mother and aunt disappeared in the sea of people. He turned his attention to Wednesday. "Do I even want to know what that was all about?" Alexander folded his arms across his chest.

"Not really," she replied.

"Yet you *are* going to tell me."

"Yes!" China raised her arms above her head. "I won… again." Spending a couple of hours playing mind-numbing arcade and carnival-type games was just what the doctor ordered, China decided.

"Yep, you sure did." Jackson smiled. "I must say, I've never been to a company picnic like this before. Food served nonstop with waiters and waitresses taking care of you."

"I'm not sure anyone has events like ours. Victoria and Elizabeth are pretty extravagant with their gifts to their employees."

"Really?"

"Last Christmas everyone who worked all year, and I mean all three hundred–plus employees, got a fifty-thousand-dollar bonus. Anyone who worked less, but over their ninety-day probationary period, got ten thousand dollars."

Jackson's eyes widened. "Seriously?"

"Yes, sir. That's why these claims that the Kingsleys don't care about the environment or their employees are so ridiculous." China shook her head.

"How's the case going, anyway?" Jackson asked.

"From what I understand, they're getting close to finding out who's behind all this nonsense."

"Good." Jackson reached for China's hand. "Maybe once this is all cleared up we can take a minivacation."

"Jackson—"

"Before you say no, let me finish, please." China nodded. Out of the corner of her eye she could see Alexander standing with Wednesday and another tall, dark-skinned man she didn't recognize. *Stay focused, China...stay with Jackson.* "You've been so focused on clearing your company's name that we haven't been able to move our relationship forward. I'd like to take you away for a few days so we can focus on us." Jackson gifted her with a sexy smile and China suddenly felt nauseous; the room started to spin.

"I think I should sit down," China whispered, trying desperately not to attract too much attention.

Jackson led her to a nearby table and helped her to sit down. "Are you all right?"

China offered up a weak smile. "Yes, I just need to eat something. I skipped breakfast." *It might be time to schedule that doctor's appointment, China.*

Jackson gestured for the waiter walking around offering bottled water. "Thank you," he said, accepting two bottles. He handed one to China. "Drink some of this."

China took a few sips. "Thanks."

"Stay put and I'll go make us a plate. Do you want anything in particular? They seem to have everything."

"Barbecue would be great," China said.

"Got it. I'll be right back." Jackson kissed her on the cheek.

"Thank you." China eyed Jackson as he went and stood in the food line. He didn't seem to notice all the women admiring him as he held a conversation with one of their engineers. "What the hell are you going to do about Jackson, China?" she murmured.

"I think I can help you with that," Wednesday offered.

Chapter 20

"Wednesday." China's brows drew together.

"May I join you?" she asked, using her hand to gesture at the empty chair across from China.

China glanced to her right at the empty table next to her. "Sure."

Wednesday smirked before taking a seat. "Thank you."

"What can I do for you?"

"Actually, it's what I can do for you. I overheard you talking to yourself," Wednesday confessed.

"You did?" China dropped her eyes for a moment, feeling embarrassed.

"Yes, and I think after you hear what I have to tell you, whatever decision you need to make about Dr. Weatherly will be clear." Wednesday waved at someone China couldn't see.

China folded her arms across her chest. "Please do share."

Wednesday looked past China and smiled. She rose from her chair. "First, I'd like for you to meet a couple of people."

China turned and saw the tall, handsome, dark-skinned man she'd seen earlier approaching, holding a toddler who was the spitting image of Wednesday. China stood as Wednesday reached for the child. "China Edwards, this is Allen Carter, my husband, and this little guy is Allen Junior. We call him AJ." Wednesday kissed the giggling child.

"Pleased to meet you." China knew her face had to be a bright shade of red. "Oh, my, what a handsome little guy."

"Nice to meet you, as well. I've heard some really wonderful things about you," Allen said.

"That's really hard to believe," she said on a nervous laugh.

"Sweetheart, can you feed AJ and I'll join you in a little bit? China and I have a little business to discuss."

"Sure." He kissed Wednesday before walking away with their son holding tight to his neck.

Wednesday returned to her chair, smiling and waving at nearby partygoers. She sat down and crossed her legs. "Surprised? I don't wear my wedding ring when I'm working."

"Very. I thought—"

"You thought Alexander and I were sleeping together." China held Wednesday's gaze as she remained silent, but just the idea had her stomach doing flips. "You don't have to admit it. In fact, I led you to believe that we were," Wednesday confessed.

"Why?"

"The short answer? It was prudent for the investigation," she said, shrugging.

"How about the long answer?" China was desperate for

more information. It was like she needed confirmation that what she was hearing was true.

"As an investigator, until I know what we're getting into, what role we need to play, I have to keep my cards close to the vest. Once I realized that we were at a point where I needed to be more embedded in the company than I'd initially thought, I needed a cover that wouldn't raise too many eyebrows. I knew my relationship with all key members of the organization had to be defined."

"So…" China's eyebrows raised.

Wednesday leaned forward. "Others within the organization needed to believe that I was sleeping with Alexander, and while that may have been uncomfortable for you, it allowed me to get close to certain people without raising suspicion. I was just one of the many consultants working here, and another one of Alexander's women, which gave me license to roam wherever I needed." Wednesday offered a quick wave of her right hand. "Let's face it, he has a pretty extensive reputation for having affairs with his consultants."

China rolled her eyes. "He had one affair with one consultant he'd dated in the past." She held up her left index finger. "Anything else you may have heard was all rumors."

"I thought we discussed truth and rumors already," Wednesday reminded China.

"Why couldn't I know what was really going on?"

Wednesday shrugged. "That's just how I work."

"Why tell me now?"

"Ultimately, I work for Victoria." She sat back in her chair. "That fact has been made perfectly clear to me and my bosses, and she wanted you to know."

China laughed. "I don't doubt that."

"Now that that's all clear, I think I better go help my husband wrangle AJ." Wednesday started to rise.

"Wait. What makes you think that your revelation would make any difference to what I have going on with Jackson?" China's eyes searched the food line to find that Jackson was heading back to the table holding two full plates.

Wednesday smirked. "You don't have to be smarter than a fifth grader to see how crazy you two are about each other, and I'm certainly not talking about you and—"

"Jackson," China said.

"Sorry for the delay." He placed a plate of food in front of China and the other in front of the empty chair next to hers.

"Jackson, you remember Wednesday," she said.

"Yes, of course. It's nice to see you again. Care to join us?" he offered.

"No, thank you. I must go find my family. Have fun." Wednesday stood and stepped away.

"Everything okay?" Jackson asked.

China plastered on the best fake smile that she could; she didn't want to draw any attention to herself. "I'm fine. This looks really good." She picked up her fork and started surveying her food.

"It does. So, did you think about my suggestion?"

You can do this. "Actually I have, and I think we should talk." She looked around the area. "This isn't exactly the best place for a serious discussion."

"It can wait for a more appropriate time and place," he said, smiling. "Until then, how about, after we eat, you give me a rematch in the arcade?"

China covered her mouth and laughed. "You got it."

"Man, Aunt Liz is dominating in skee ball. That arcade tent was a great idea. All of our guys love it, especially after being out on the rigs for so long. You want to go shoot some hoops?" Morgan asked, taking a seat next to Alexander and handing him a bottle of beer.

"No," Alexander said, accepting the bottle. "Thanks."

"What's up with you?" Morgan followed Alexander's menacing look. "Oh, I see."

"You see what?"

"I see you still haven't manned up and told China what we already know." Alexander took a long pull from his beer bottle. "So, what, you just going to sit here and stare at her from across the room?" Morgan asked.

"I have everything in my personal life under control."

"If you say so." Morgan finished off his beer.

"Is everything in place for Wednesday and her team?" Alexander asked, switching topics.

"Yep, everything's ready and they have full access."

"Good. The sooner we end this, the better." Alexander checked his watch and pulled out his phone.

"Agreed. I still find it hard to believe that Tammy's involved."

"She's not, and this will prove it," Alexander defended his assistant.

"And if it doesn't?"

"We'll deal with it," Alexander promised.

Victoria returned to the DJ booth and took the microphone. "Good evening. Is everyone having a good time?"

The crowd responded with a boisterous cheer and Victoria's face lit up, which made Alexander smile. "Well, it's about that time."

"What's she talking about?" Morgan asked.

"Wait for it," Alexander advised, smiling and nodding.

"Grab your partner. The dance floor will be open for business in ten minutes. It's time for our annual two-step contest."

"I feel you on that move, getting China out on the dance floor, but if you don't want someone else to beat you to the punch—" Morgan pointed in the direction of where China and Jackson stood talking "—I suggest you get moving."

"No need to rush," he said, hoping he was right.

Morgan gave him a doubtful look. "You that confident?"

"No, actually I'm not. I'm just hoping she'll want to dance with me." His tone softened. "Here goes nothing."

Alexander crossed the dance floor, ignoring requests for his attention and keeping his eyes on his target. He knew his behavior garnered some attention, but he didn't care. Alexander wasn't a man who feared much, yet the closer he got to China, the more he realized what the answer to this one question meant to him. His heart was beating so fast, pushing blood through his veins, that Alexander just knew he could break out into an old-school cartoon-character-style run.

"Alexander," China said as he approached. "You okay?"

"Yes." A corner of his mouth turned up. "Hello, Jackson." Alexander offered his hand.

As the two men shook hands, China gifted Alexander with a familiar smile. It was the smile that said she appreciated his effort, even though she knew it was killing him to make it.

"Jackson, I hope you don't mind if I borrow China for a bit. We have a title to defend." Alexander trained his eyes on the surprised look on China's face. He could almost see the wheels turning; she remembered.

"Our title," China whispered.

"Title?" Jackson questioned. frowning.

"Yes. We won the dance contest last year. We did the—"

"Two-step," she murmured, staring up at Alexander.

"All right, everyone. The first category in the dance

contest is the two-step," the DJ announced. "Will our defending champions please take the dance floor?"

"Shall we?" Alexander offered China his hand.

Chapter 21

China's eyes roamed Alexander's face, and doubt clouded his handsome features as he stood still as a statue, waiting for her response. Everything and everyone just seemed to fade away as desire and a need to assuage his concerns began to rise within China; these were easily evoked when he trained his eyes on her.

It's just a dance, China tried to convince herself as she placed the palm of her hand in his and rose in silence. Alexander snaked his free arm around her waist and escorted her onto the dance floor. Having Alexander's hands on her body was making it difficult for China to concentrate.

"Breathe, China," Alexander whispered. "We've got this."

China released a quick breath. "I hope I remember the steps."

"I got you," he promised. "Just follow my lead."

China grinned up at him. "Like always."

The soulful sound of Babyface's "Exceptional" began to waft through the air. China placed the palm of her left hand on his shoulder as Alexander placed his right hand on the small of her back. Their opposite hands were extended out at their sides and locked. "Let's show these folks our Texas version of the Chicago two-step."

China laughed as Alexander led her in slow, sensual steps across the floor, exhibiting one-hand swing outs, double turns and several sexy lifts and dips. She blocked out the roar of the crowd. All China could see was the way Alexander looked at her, how his eyes lit up with each suggestive move of her hips, which she rewarded with a sexy smile. There was so much more going on between them than a simple dance. Something neither of them had been willing to address. As their dance came to an end, China felt a sense of loss that she was determined wouldn't last long.

They took their bows and walked to the side of the dance floor, where China was met by Jackson. "That was something else," he said, handing her a bottle of water and offering one to Alexander, which he declined with a shake of his head and hand.

"Thank you." She twisted off the top of the bottle and took several sips.

"Very sexy," Jackson added, shoving his hands in his pockets, a move that she could see sparked Alexander's attention; he stuck his nose in the air.

"It was just a dance, Jackson," China defended herself as she felt Alexander's eyes bore into the side of her face. While she knew Alexander would take her statement the wrong way, she didn't want to escalate the situation. It was a very sexy dance and the public intimacy they'd just shared reaffirmed what her heart already knew; she loved and wanted Alexander and she had to tell Jackson. Yet now wasn't the time or place to make any formal declarations.

Jackson dropped his shoulders, removed his hands from his pockets and intertwined his hands with China's, bringing them to his lips. "You're right, sweetheart."

Alexander's face went blank. "Yes, it was just a dance," he echoed.

"Excuse us," Brice interrupted with Morgan standing at his side. "We need to get back to the office."

"Why? What's going on?" China asked, pulling her hands free; her eyes swerved between the brothers.

"There's been a development in the case," Brice explained.

"Okay, let me—"

"No. We've got this," Alexander declared, turning on his heel and heading toward the parking lot.

"Alex," China whispered, taking a small step forward. She knew he was more than angry—he was hurt and most likely felt betrayed, too, and she hated it.

Brice and Morgan looked at each other before turning their sights on China. "We'll keep you posted," Brice promised before leaving to follow Alexander.

"How about we get out of here?" Jackson asked, smiling.

China sighed. "Jackson, this isn't going to work. I think you're a wonderful man with a big heart and you will make some woman feel very lucky to have you."

Jackson's shoulders dropped. "You're just not that woman."

"Wait up, man," Morgan yelled after Alexander.

"Catch up," Alexander responded over his shoulder.

Alexander stopped next to his truck with his arms

folded across his chest. "Looks like you two need to get back in the gym," he told Brice.

"What...the hell...was that?" Brice asked between breaths.

"Seriously, dude, Alexander's right. You need to spend more time working out," Morgan interjected, grimacing at his brother.

"We all can't spend our time working in plants and on rigs where we're outside putting in hours of manual labor," Brice countered.

"Seriously, what was that all about back there?" Morgan asked Alexander.

"What?" Alexander replied, knowing exactly what his brother meant.

"That shot you took back there," Morgan clarified.

Alexander shook his head. "No shot. I just don't need her on this. We got it covered." The words made him sick to even say.

"I see," Brice said, nodding.

"Now I get it. What happened?" Morgan asked.

"Everything looked cool when you two were on the dance floor. More than cool, in fact. Pretty damn hot," Brice responded.

"We don't have time for this." Alexander pulled out his keys.

Morgan snatched the keys from Alexander's hand. "Yes, we do. You're not going into the office with your head all messed up."

"Give me my damn keys, Morgan!" Alexander demanded through gritted teeth, taking a step closer to his brother.

"Chill," Brice said, stepping between the two men. "We aren't those kids anymore. We don't fight through our issues. We have over three hundred employees and their families mere yards away."

Morgan took a step back. "I guess we shouldn't let our employees see us beating the hell out of each other."

"Not to mention Mom and Aunt Elizabeth," Brice added.

"Sorry," Alexander said, before turning his back to his brothers and slamming his right palm on the roof of his truck. "Dammit."

"What happened?" Brice asked.

"She made her choice," Alexander said. He turned and leaned back against his truck's door.

Morgan frowned. "When?"

"She told Old Boy it was just a dance," Alexander explained.

Brice's eyebrows stood at attention. "No way *that* was just a dance."

"Yeah, well, I guess he means more to her than I realized," Alexander said, pushing past the lump in his throat.

"Or maybe you're making more out of her statement than you should," Morgan advised.

"I know her better than anyone…remember?" Alexander reminded his brothers. "Can I have my keys now? We need to get to the office."

"Look, man, I know you're feeling some kind of way right now, but I wouldn't close that door just yet," Brice advised.

Morgan handed Alexander his keys. "Just try not to lose it when we get to the office. The sooner we find out who's behind all this mess, the sooner things can get back to normal."

Morgan and Brice left to find their own vehicles. "Normal," Alexander said, looking back in the direction of where he had left China. "What's normal?"

* * *

China and Jackson had moved away from the crowd to the smaller tent that had been designated as a relaxation lounge. Various styles of seating had been set up, along with a self-service bar. China sat on a white sofa next to Jackson with her hands resting in her lap.

"You sure about this?" Jackson asked, his jaw clenched.

"Yes, I'm very sure, and I'm sorry," China replied.

"Do you think he'll be able to give you what you need?" Doubt, and maybe even sympathy, marred his face.

China looked past Jackson, out at the crowd of people dancing and enjoying themselves, and she smiled. She looked back at Jackson and said, "I have no idea. What I do know is, if I don't try and figure out this thing between me and Alexander, I'll regret it."

Jackson stood. "Then I think you should do what you have to do."

"Thank you."

Jackson leaned down and kissed China on the forehead. "Take care of yourself," he said before turning to leave.

"Now what, China?" she questioned, resting her head against the back of the sofa.

"There you are," Joyce called out, walking into the tent and over to her friend.

China raised her head. "Here I am."

"What's up?" Joyce took a sip of the wine she held.

"Nothing."

"Where is handsome going? I saw him heading toward the parking lot."

"Home, I suspect," China said.

"Home? Girl, you better stop tripping and sign on the dotted line with that man, if you know what I mean."

"I do and I can't." China laid her head back again.

"Why the hell not?" Joyce finished off her wine.

"It's complicated," China murmured.

"The only thing I'd find complicated about that man is if I had another one just like him." Joyce giggled.

China rolled her head to the side and stared at her friend in silence.

"No way. You've been holding out on your girl. Spill. You got another man?" Joyce moved over to the bar and refilled her wine glass.

"Not exactly. I told you, it's complicated."

"Don't sweat it. The only real complication you could ever have is if you finally hooked up with Alexander, and don't bother trying to deny the attraction between you two," she laughed as she returned to her seat. "Now that's a complication."

China sat up and dropped her face into the palms of her hands. "Like I said, complicated," she murmured.

"Finally…"

China dropped her hands. "You really aren't shocked."

"Of course not. I figured it was only a matter of time."

China pushed a wayward piece of hair behind her ear. "Porsche was. In fact, she thinks the whole idea of me and Alexander is gross."

"She would. You know that girl's got a thing for Alexander, right?"

"What? You think Porsche wants Alexander? No way," China said, laughing. "You couldn't be further from the truth."

"Yes, way," Joyce said, nodding. "I've seen the looks she's given him. There's most certainly something going on there."

"Not what you think. The only thing Porsche feels for Alexander is tolerance, which is good, considering how much she really dislikes him," China explained.

"How can you be so sure?" Joyce's mouth set in a hard line.

"Because I've met her *girlfriend* who she's madly in love with," China informed Joyce.

"Oh, I didn't get that vibe. So, what are you going to do about Alexander?"

China got to her feet. "I'm going to the office to talk to him."

Joyce downed the last of her wine and placed the glass on one of the side tables. "He's at the office? Good, I'll go with you."

"What happened to spending time with Lester? You two looked pretty cozy out on the dance floor earlier."

"We are…we were, and I am," she said, chuckling so hard she snorted. "He had to go by the office."

"How much wine have you had?" China asked, smiling and giving her friend the once-over.

"Only a few bottles…I mean glasses," she giggled.

China shook her head. "Why is Lester at the office?"

"Ben called and told him that his car was ready, so he rode back to the office with a couple of guys to go pick it up. He didn't want me to miss all the fun. This will make it easier to get me and save him from having to come back and pick me up. We'll miss the fireworks show, but we can make our own," she said, wiggling her eyebrows. "I'll text him."

China smiled, feeling a bit envious of her friend. She had no idea how Alexander was going to respond to seeing her or what she had to say, but China was determined to make him listen. "I'm really happy for you."

"I'm happy for us both." Joyce looped their arms. "Now, let's go get our men."

Chapter 22

China laughed as they made their way back to the car. Joyce's explanation of how she'd distracted Lester in the game tent so she could beat him at darts, and the fact that he had two left feet on the dance floor, was a welcome distraction. Listening to Joyce and her antics got China out of her head about what might happen when she finally reached Alexander.

"You sure we parked in the right section?" Joyce's eyes scanned the area.

"I'm sure." China hit the key fob and the car's headlights blinked. "See?"

"Can I—"

"No, you still can't drive Alexander's car. Anyway, you've been drinking, remember."

"Oh, yeah," Joyce replied, releasing a loud cackle.

They got into the car and secured themselves with their seat belts before China pulled out of the parking space.

"You sure you know how to get back to the freeway? It's getting dark and all these trees aren't helping."

"Of course. It's a straight shot down one road to the highway, and it's not that dark. Besides, there are lights along the way."

"Yeah, a long-ass two-lane road with the lights spread far apart." Joyce hit a switch and her seat reclined. "Wake me when we get there."

"No problem," China said, snickering, as she turned onto the long stretch of highway.

China wouldn't dare admit it to Joyce, but she *was* a little nervous driving on such an isolated road in the dark, especially since the streetlights barely lit her path. She breathed a sigh of relief when she soon saw a set of headlights following her. The road only led to and from the private park that the company rented out for the picnic, so she was sure she was now traveling down the lonely road with a fellow employee.

"You might want to slow down," she said to the dark van, which was fast approaching in her rearview mirror.

Soon the van was at her side, attempting to pass. China lifted her foot from the accelerator in order to assist in his efforts. Only the driver, whom she couldn't see clearly, must have had another agenda. He rammed his van into the car, jerking China and jarring Joyce awake.

"What the…!" China yelled, gripping the steering wheel and instantly fearful of what could happen next when Alexander's face flashed through her mind.

"What happened?" Joyce grabbed the dashboard.

"This guy hit—"

Before she could finish her statement, they were hit again. Both women screamed and China accelerated. "Call for help," she ordered, but before Joyce could react, the van hit the back half of the car, sending it spinning out of control.

* * *

Alexander and his brothers walked into their conference room to find Wednesday talking to his mother and Meeks Montgomery. "This must be big if we got the big boss out late on a Saturday night," Alexander said, offering his hand.

Meeks shook Alexander's hand and replied, "No, she's home with our triplets. You'll just have to settle for me."

Everyone laughed as both Brice and Morgan shook Meeks's hand. "Where's China?" Victoria asked, glaring back at the door.

Morgan looked over at Alexander. "You want to take this one?"

Alexander gave Morgan the evil eye. "I told China we had it and that we would keep her posted."

"Actually, I told her that," Brice corrected.

Alexander ignored his brother's comments. "We'll fill her in later," he said, still reeling from the sting of her rejection. Not even the look of confusion on his mother's face could temper the hurricane of emotions Alexander was navigating at that moment. "Let's get started. I hate to keep you away from your family too long," Alexander said to Meeks.

"Yes, let's," Victoria echoed.

Everyone took a seat at the conference table except Wednesday. She stood at the front of the room and began to explain what they'd finally uncovered. "After Sam dropped Tammy off at home, he and Morris Henderson came to the office. Sam used Tammy's keys to get into the building and Alexander's access codes to get on to the executive floor—"

"You're sure it wasn't Tammy using her own keys and codes?" Morgan questioned with a frown.

"I told you, Tammy wouldn't do this," Alexander defended her. *I'm not losing China and my assistant in the same day.*

"We're sure," she said to Morgan. "Tammy has solid alibis for all the times in question."

"In fact, all but the three people we suspected and have had under surveillance can be accounted for," Meeks explained.

"Cut to the chase. Who's responsible for this mess?" Alexander demanded, the volume of his voice escalated.

"Please excuse my son's rudeness. We have a lot riding on this investigation," Victoria explained.

"Trust me, I completely understand. Wednesday," Meeks said, gesturing with a nod of his head for her to proceed.

Wednesday returned the nod. "We believe Evan Perez is the mastermind behind this whole thing, but we can't prove it," she informed them.

"We can't prove it *yet*," Meeks corrected.

Victoria's face hardened. "Evan Perez has been trying to take our company down for years. He hates us. He doesn't think women can handle this level of responsibility and shouldn't be the head of such a prominent organization, especially one in this industry."

"Well, he'd better stay the hell away from my wife and her sister," Meeks said, clearly trying to lighten the mood.

Morgan shook his head and frowned. "I don't understand. Companies lose business deals to each other all the time—it's called competition. This almost seems personal."

A look passed between Meeks and Wednesday. "What... what is it?" Alexander asked.

"Mrs. Kingsley, would you like for us to explain the potential motive?" Meeks asked.

All eyes landed on Victoria. "No," she said, rising from

her seat. She walked over to the bar, poured herself a shot of whiskey and tossed it back.

"Mother…" Brice called.

"This fight has little to do with business," Victoria said with her back to everyone.

"Why?" Alexander asked.

Victoria turned and faced her family. "After your father died—"

"This is about you," Alexander concluded.

"What, he came on to you, didn't he?" Morgan asked, folding his arms across his chest.

"Actually it wasn't me who he hit on," she explained, frowning. "After your Uncle Harrison died, Liz fell into a deep depression for quite some time."

"That was a difficult time for us all, Mother," Morgan reminded.

Victoria offered up a weak smile and returned to her chair. "Once Liz started to pull through the depression, she started to live again—work, attend social events and see friends."

"Was Perez one of those friends?" Alexander asked.

Victoria nodded. "But not in the way he wanted. When she rejected him, he crossed a line he shouldn't have."

"What!" Alexander and Morgan chorused, standing so fast it sent their chairs to the floor.

Brice remained seated with his hands fisted on the conference table. "Did he hurt her?"

Victoria rose from her chair and started pacing the room. "Calm down, boys. No, Perez didn't hurt her."

Alexander and Morgan picked up their chairs and sat back down. "What happened?"

"I told you. He crossed a line that he shouldn't have, one that I reminded him both physically and financially he should never cross again."

"Do I want to know what that means?" Alexander asked, frowning.

Victoria's expression dulled. "All you need to know is that I've done a number of things to protect, and when necessary, avenge my family. So yes, Morgan, Evan Perez's actions against me and our company are very personal."

"Okay, so what can you prove?" Alexander asked Meeks.

"We can prove that your initial, EPA-approved disposal policy and procedures were entered into your system appropriately and then were changed without your knowledge by Sam Thompson—the brother of your HR manager. He used Tammy to gain access to you and your information."

Wednesday pulled out two legal documents. "We have signed affidavits from Sam's sister, Terri Thompson, and Sharon Doyle, the records manager, stating that they were both paid to sabotage your company and to give misleading statements to the EPA."

"You should know, Mrs. Kingsley, that Sam and Terri's motives for helping Perez are very different than Sharon's, and it's laid out in the affidavits," Meeks informed.

Victoria nodded but remained silent.

"What are the motives?" Brice asked.

"Sam and Terri's father worked at Evan Perez's first company. He was a part of his executive team. Victoria bankrupted the company and their father lost a lot of money. Recruiting them to help bring Victoria down was easy."

"How did you get them to confess…and in writing, too?" Morgan frowned, his surprise clear.

"Wednesday is very good at her job," Meeks praised her.

"I was hired and trained by the best," she proclaimed.

"Yes, my wife and her sister, Farrah," Meeks clarified.

Everyone laughed. "I just explained their precarious legal position," Wednesday offered.

"It appears Ms. Doyle is ready to roll over on Perez, too," Meeks said.

"Sharon actually believed he was going to leave his wife and marry her. Unfortunately, she doesn't have any direct proof of his involvement," Wednesday said. "She's blaming everything on Terri and her brother, and we do have tons of evidence against them."

Alexander reached for the document and started reading through it. He immediately thought that if China were there she would have read the affidavits in less than a minute. "She actually admits to providing misleading and exaggerated statements to the EPA and helping Sam change documents. She's even confessed to pulling copies of operations meeting notes so that they had enough information to support their claims." Alexander shook his head, tossed the documents on the table and started rubbing his right knuckles in his left hand. He met Morgan's gaze.

"Where's Sam right now?" Morgan asked, mimicking his brother's hand gesture.

"We have him under digital surveillance," she said.

"How?" Alexander asked.

"He has a weakness for very pretty women and Rolex watches," Meeks shared.

"What?" Morgan scratched his head.

"We had one of our agents meet Sam at a bar and engage him in conversation. She convinced him that her boyfriend cheated on her, and to get back at him, she was going to sell his vintage Rolex watch for one hundred dollars. He took the bait."

Brice and Morgan stood with bewildered looks on their faces. Alexander shook his head. "Guys, the watch had a bug in it."

"Oh…nice move," Morgan complimented the team.

"We can pick them up and turn them over to the police for breaking into the office tonight but—"

"But what?" Alexander and Morgan chorused.

"Do we know why they broke in? What was he after?" Brice added.

"We have no idea. Before we left the office we planted the story about upgrading the systems to see if he'd bite, and he did. Only right after Sam and Morris broke into the office tonight, they turned around and left. They got a call on a burner cell phone so we couldn't trace it. Whoever it was must have really spooked them."

"I wonder why," Brice mused, his eyes roaming the room.

"We're not sure," Meeks said. "We can turn Sam in, but he'll just make bail and take off."

"What do you suggest?" Victoria asked.

"Keep them under surveillance for now. Just until you get the EPA off your backs. Maybe he'll lead us to evidence that can implicate Perez or lead us to someone who can," Meeks recommended.

"I agree." Victoria nodded.

"Now all China has to do is incorporate this new information into our response," Alexander said, fighting the urge to call her. China was always the first person he thought of whenever he had any type of news he needed to share.

"Kristen can schedule a press conference right away," Brice said.

Victoria pulled out her phone and started dialing. "I have to make a few calls. I need for our evidence to get the proper attention it deserves." She rose from her seat and walked to the other side of the room.

"How's Tammy?" Alexander asked Wednesday.

"She's upset and blaming herself," Wednesday explained. "She thinks she should have seen through Sam and all his manipulations. She's having a hard time dealing with the fact that Sam pretended to care about her."

Alexander stood and headed toward the door. "I should go talk to her."

"Wait. I think you should give her some space," Wednesday suggested.

Victoria walked over to where Alexander and Wednesday were standing. "Excuse me." Victoria turned and faced her son. "Alexander, I can't reach China," she said, holding her cell phone.

Wednesday and Meeks's phones rang at the same moment. They both excused themselves from the room to take their respective calls. Alexander tamped down the hurt that was trying to surface and checked his watch. "I'm sure they're enjoying the last of the fireworks. That, or they've already headed home."

"They?" Victoria's brows came together.

Alexander's mouth twisted. "The man she's seeing."

"Oh…"

Wednesday walked back into the conference room with Meeks on her heels. "Excuse me, Victoria. Alexander, I'm sorry, but China's been in a car accident."

Alexander heard the collective gasps, but his mind and body were starting to shut down. Meeks slowly approached Alexander with his hands raised slightly out in front of him as if he was approaching a volatile situation. Alexander's face went blank and his lungs stopped working; he was instantly overtaken by fear.

Meeks peered into his eyes and said, "Alexander, I need you to listen to me. I know where your head's at right now. Believe me, I've been there. Focus on the sound of my voice. I need you to breathe."

Alexander released a quick breath, blinked twice before inhaling and releasing another breath slowly. "China…is she…alive?" he whispered.

"Yes, but that's all I know. They were taken to Methodist," Meeks informed everyone.

"They? Who was in the car with her?" Victoria asked.

"Joyce… Joyce was with her," Wednesday said.

Morgan pulled out his keys. "I'll drive."

Alexander regained his equanimity. "Pull Joyce's personnel file. You'll find her emergency contact information there, and call Lester. He should know what's going on," he ordered.

"What about China? I know she doesn't have any immediate family, but is there anyone we should notify?" Wednesday asked.

Alexander surveyed all the worried faces in the room. "You already have. I'm her family."

Chapter 23

"Hmm…" China felt as if she was being held down. She was having trouble breathing and she saw flashes of light, even though she couldn't make her eyes work.

"Ms. Edwards… Ms. China Edwards, can you open your eyes for me?"

China fought through the haze and slowly opened her eyes. She scanned the room. The strange bed, the sight of unfamiliar faces hovering over her, and the beeping sounds of machines made her feel anxious. *Why am I in a hospital?* "That's it. Welcome back," an unfamiliar voice said.

China tried to sit up but couldn't; she felt so heavy and she ached all over. She opened her mouth to speak but closed it quickly. *What happened?* "I'm Dr. Jafar, and that's your nurse, Jimmy."

Jimmy started checking her vital signs. "We're going to take good care of you," he promised.

"You're at Methodist Hospital. There was a car accident, but you're going to be fine."

China fought to make her voice work. She swallowed and cleared her throat. "Doctor, how's my friend?" she whispered.

"The woman in the car with you? I can't give you any specifics on her condition, but I can tell you that she, too, will be okay."

China offered up a weak smile as tears rolled down her face.

"You're both very lucky. I understand from the paramedics that had your car hit the tree from a different angle, we'd be having a very different conversation."

"What's wrong with me?"

"You have a couple of bruised ribs, a mild concussion." He used a penlight to check her pupils as he spoke. "And a few cuts and bruises. I want to run a couple more tests, and I'm waiting for your blood work to come back, but like I said, you'll be just fine." He made notes in her chart as he stood next to the bed. "Are you experiencing any cramping or pain in your abdomen?"

"A little, maybe… I'm not sure how I feel, actually."

"On a scale of one to ten, how's the pain rate?"

"A six, I guess," she said.

"I ordered you a mild pain reliever that Jimmy's about to administer, but once I have a few more test results in, I'll give you something a little stronger."

Nurse Jimmy came over and injected the medicine into her IV.

"I need to make a call," she murmured, instantly feeling the effects of the medicine. While she understood what the doctor was telling her and appreciated his encouraging words, China was scared, hurting and couldn't handle this alone. "Please, give me a phone."

The door to China's hospital room opened slowly and Alexander crossed the threshold. The fear on his handsome face made her want to comfort him. "Alex," she whispered, and in spite of the discomfort, China raised her arm and extended her hand. Alexander was at her side in three strides.

He wrapped his hand around hers, leaned down and gently kissed her on the lips. "Thank God you're alive. I don't know what I would've done if…"

China smiled as her tears really started to flow. "Thank God you're here." Alexander kissed her again and wiped away her tears.

"Excuse me, sir." Dr. Jafar started to speak, but Alexander held up his hand, instructing the doctor to stop talking.

"Are you okay?" he whispered.

"They tell me I am. My head and ribs hurt, and I'm pretty sore, too."

Alexander turned his attention to the doctor. "Can you give her something for the pain?"

The doctor looked at China. "It's okay, doctor, this is my…family, Alexander Kingsley. You can tell him everything. Alexander, this is Dr. Jafar."

The doctor nodded. "We have, and we will increase her dose as soon as we get a couple more test results back."

"It's okay, Alex." China squeezed his hand.

"I was so worried," he admitted, kissing the palm of her hand.

"Me, too. Have you checked in on Joyce?"

"No, but Mom did and Lester is there, too," he shared.

"That's good." China felt a sense of relief; accident or not, she hated the thought that she could have seriously injured her friend.

"I'll be right back," the doctor said before he and Jimmy left the room.

"Do you remember what happened?" Alexander asked.

"Vaguely. We were on our way to the office," she started explaining, adjusting her body and wincing with each attempt. "When—"

"Wait, you were coming to the office, why?" His forehead creased.

China squeezed his hand. "To find you," she said, staring into his eyes.

"Me, why?"

"Kiss me, Alex," China whispered.

The corners of Alexander's mouth rose. He stood, hovered over China and said, "You're so gorgeous." Alexander kissed her on the lips with more passion and purpose than he intended in that instance. China knew they had a lot to discuss but all she could think about was how happy she was to be with Alexander.

China smiled. "I was coming to tell—"

"Excuse me, Ms. Edwards," Dr. Jafar said as he entered the room holding her chart. "We have those final results."

Nurse Jimmy came into the room pushing a machine that he placed on the right side of China's bed. "What's going on?" Alexander asked, straightening to his full height.

"China, I have a delicate matter to discuss with you. Are you sure you want to talk in front of Mr. Kingsley?"

"It's okay. What's wrong?" she asked, her features twisting with concern.

"Did you know that you are pregnant?" he asked, staring down at her.

China's face went blank. "What?" Her body began to shake.

Alexander offered a supportive squeeze of China's right hand while gripping the bedside rails with his left. China looked up to see that his expression had dulled. "That's not possible. I mean…I know it's possible, but I had my cycle last month."

Alexander released her hand and the bed rail, and took a step back as the nurse came around to his side to check her IVs. "Was it normal?" Dr. Jafar asked.

"It was light, but I guess it was normal. I had a virus, too, so I really don't know." China was overwhelmed by emotions as the realization of what he'd said started to take root. She was filled with disbelief, excitement and hope.

"This ultrasound will tell us roughly how far along you are," the doctor explained. He placed a clear warm gel on her stomach and rolled the Doppler across her lower abdomen.

"Alex…"

"I'm here," he replied, his tone flat. He hadn't moved from his spot where he had a clear view of the screen.

"There's your baby," the doctor said, pointing to the small figure on the screen. "There's his heart and, as you can see and hear, it's beating nice and fast, just as it should be. So far, he looks perfect."

"He?" Alexander said.

"Sorry, it's too early to determine the sex. That's just a force of habit," the doctor replied, looking at Alexander. He turned his attention back to China, who was crying. "You appear to be about seven weeks."

China felt unspeakable joy. She had never experienced anything like it before. There was only one thing that could make the moment perfect, but before she could act the doctor asked, "How's the cramping?"

"Mild," she replied, fear creeping up her spine.

"What's wrong, Doctor?" Alexander inquired, still unmoving and emotionless.

"The risk is minimal, but we want to spend the next twenty-four hours watching for a miscarriage, which is why I can't give you any additional pain meds. You need to be able to tell us what's happening with your body."

China's breath caught. "A spontaneous miscarriage."

"Your body suffered a lot of trauma in the accident. Jimmy is going to hook you up to the fetal monitor so we can make sure your baby continues to be okay. Don't worry. This is all just a precaution."

"Thank you," China whispered, wiping away a fresh batch of tears. She was experiencing an avalanche of feelings, with fear being the dominating emotion.

After hooking China up to the baby monitor and lowering the volume on the machine, Dr. Jafar and Jimmy excused themselves. Alexander came and stood next to China's bed with his hands in his pocket. "Would you like me to call Jackson for you?" Alexander's mouth was set in a hard line.

"Jackson?" Her brows snapped together.

"Yes, Jackson."

Realization finally set in and China sighed. "No. Alex, you don't need to call Jackson. He's not the father of my baby. You are," she declared.

Alexander had felt as if he'd been hit by a stun gun when the doctor announced China's pregnancy. He'd thought their reconnection was over and his heart was breaking all over again; all he wanted to do was get the hell out of there. Yet he knew he had to be there for his friend. Now this magnificent creature, the woman he loved more than anything, was telling him she was carrying his child and all he could do was stare at her.

China held his gaze. "I never slept with Jackson—or anyone else since we made love. I couldn't. Even before then it had been nearly two years. You know that. You asked me why I came looking for you."

Alexander nodded; he was experiencing too many emotions to speak.

"I came to tell you that I'd ended things with Jackson because I was in love with you. I think I've been in love with you for a really long time. I came to tell you that I wanted to give us a chance. That I wanted to have your child someday. I know having a child wasn't part of your plan, but I'm so very happy and I know in my heart everything is going to be okay with this baby. Please say something."

Alexander pushed out a breath and sat down. He took her hands in his and kissed both palms. "I'm in love with you, too, China. I think I've been in love with you from the beginning of our friendship but only really acknowledged it recently."

"Really?" China's whole face lit up.

"Really." He leaned over and devoured her mouth as though he'd never get another chance to kiss her. He pressed his forehead against hers. "I want our child more than anything, too, my love."

China threw her arms around his neck and cried. Alexander sat at China's bedside and held her until she was all cried out. Alexander was overwhelmed by the love for his new family and the strong sense of pride he felt toward his unborn child. "Did you see my son?" Alexander gifted her with a wide smile.

China laughed and winced. "Your son? It could be a girl, you know, and don't make me laugh."

"In this family…my money is on the first one being a boy."

China grinned. "First one." She yawned and placed their intertwined hands on her stomach. "We're having a baby."

"Yes, we are. You need to get some rest. I'm going to step out."

China flinched and tightened her grip on his hands. "Don't leave me."

Alexander kissed her gently on the lips. He didn't want to leave her side for even a second, but he knew if he didn't go tell everyone what was going on soon, they'd be bombarded by a concerned family, and he didn't want China getting overexcited or too stressed.

"Never, my love. I'm just stepping out to bring the family up to speed on things. Everyone's been so worried. I'll just be right down the hall and I'll be back before you know it. I promise."

"Okay," China said, closing her eyes slowly and releasing Alexander's hand.

Alexander walked out of the room, closing the door behind him. "How is she, son?" Victoria asked, worry staining her lovely face.

Alexander pulled her into a hug. "She's good…better than good, actually." Alexander released his mother and scanned the worried faces of his brothers and Wednesday. "China got a little banged up but she's going to be okay. I have some news. We're going to have a baby."

"Dude, congratulations." Morgan slapped Alexander on the back.

"I'm so happy for you, son…for you both," Victoria said.

"That's wonderful." Brice shook Alexander's hand.

"Thanks, everyone, and yes, before you all ask… Mother—" he zeroed in on her calculating stare "—I will be asking China to marry me."

"Good, then you'll need this." Victoria pulled a black ring box from her purse.

"You always carry engagement rings around in your bag, Mother?" Brice asked, laughing.

"Only when I think it may come in handy, son."

"Thanks, but no. I have something else in mind. Can I get you to help me with that?" he asked a very excited Victoria.

"Of course, darling," she replied, putting her ring away.

"Well, at least some good came from that accident," Alexander said.

"I'm sorry, Alexander, but the car crash wasn't an accident," Wednesday informed him.

"What did you say?" Alexander asked, sure he'd misheard her.

"We checked out the scene and talked to Joyce, and she stated that they were run off the road," she explained.

"My goodness," Victoria said as her left hand flew to her heart.

"We recommend beefing up security around all of you until we know what's going on."

Alexander ran back to China's room, yelling over his shoulder, "Make it happen." He opened China's hospital room door to find Jimmy checking the fetal monitor. "Is everything okay?"

"Yes, sir, just charting the results—this little one is a fighter."

"Just like his or her mother." Alexander sat in a reclining chair next to China, held her hand and watched over her for the rest of the night. He promised himself that he'd do everything in his power to keep himself as well as his family safe. They had instantly become his main priority.

Chapter 24

The next morning, China yawned and opened her eyes. She smiled as soon as their eyes met. China was happier than she ever could have imagined. She had the family and love she'd always wanted. "Hi."

"Hi, baby." Alexander rose from his seat and came to sit on the side of China's bed. "How do you feel?"

"Happy," she said, pulling his hand to her lips for a kiss.

"Me, too. Any cramping?" He brushed her hair from her face.

"No."

"That's great. The doctor told me if you weren't cramping when you woke up, everything should be fine." China watched as his face relaxed. His joy and sense of relief were overwhelming, yet she could still see how tense he was.

"What's wrong?" she asked, frowning.

"Nothing."

China narrowed her eyes. "This is me you're talking to, Alex. What's going on?"

Alexander sighed. "What do you remember about the accident?"

"Umm…we left the park and I was driving down that long road when a van…" China frowned.

"What about the van?" he pushed.

"I think they tried to pass me, and then I guess…they must have lost control because they hit us."

Alexander held her hand. "You were intentionally run off the road."

"What…why?"

"I don't know but we're going to find out, and whoever did this, we'll make them pay. I promise. The police will want to talk to you about what happened, too. In the meantime, everyone in the family's getting a little extra security."

"What does that mean?"

"Wednesday is making arrangements for us all to have twenty-four-hour protection," he explained.

"Do you really think that's necessary?" she asked. Her voice cracked as she sat up in her bed.

Alexander cupped her face with both hands and said, "Please don't worry. I'm going to keep my family safe."

"Your family." China smiled. "I like the sound of that."

"Good, because I can't wait any longer." Alexander reached into his pants pocket and pulled out a large diamond engagement ring. "I know this isn't the most romantic place but…"

China's eyes grew wide. "Alex…"

"I love you so much. In fact, I had 'Alex loves China' engraved on the inside, just in case you ever forget." He tilted the ring so she could read it. "You'll always be my baby. China Edwards, will you marry me? Please…"

China presented Alexander with a shaky left hand as tears ran down her face. "Yes…"

Alexander placed the ring on her finger and kissed her hand. He lowered his head to her stomach. "Did you hear that, baby? Mom said yes."

China laid her head back and laughed. "Alex…"

"Yes, my love."

China's whole face lit up. "We're having a baby."

* * * * *

"Now you just have to seal the deal and get to closing." He knew that just because an offer had been made didn't mean the sale was a foregone conclusion. Deals could fall apart at any time. Not that it ever happened to him. Daniel took every precaution to ensure that it didn't.

"Of course."

"Speaking of deals, I've recently signed a new client, a developer that has tasked me with selling out the eighty condos in his building in downtown Miami."

Angela's eyes grew large. "Sounds amazing."

KPEXP0517

"It is, but it's a challenge. The lower-end condos go for a thousand a square foot, and the penthouse is fifteen hundred a square foot."

"Well, if anyone can do it, you can."

Daniel appreciated her ego boost. "Thank you, but praise is not the reason I'm mentioning it."

"No?" She quirked a brow and he couldn't resist returning it with a grin.

"I want you to work on the project with me."

"You do?" Astonishment was evident in her voice.

"Why do you think I plucked you away from that other firm? It was to give you the opportunity to grow and to learn under my tutelage."

"I'm ready for whatever you want to offer me." She blushed as soon as she said the words, no doubt because he could certainly take it to mean something other than work. Something like what he could offer her in the bedroom.

Where had that thought come from?

It was his cardinal rule to never date any woman in the workplace. Angela would be no different. He didn't mix business with pleasure.

He banished the thought and finally replied, "I'm sure you are." Then he walked over to his desk, procured a folder and handed it to her. "Read this. It'll fill you in on the development. Let's plan on putting our heads together on a marketing strategy tomorrow after you've had time to digest it."

Angela nodded and walked toward the door. "And, Daniel?"

"Yes?"

"Thank you for the opportunity."

*Don't miss MIAMI AFTER HOURS
by Yahrah St. John, available June 2017
wherever Harlequin® Kimani Romance™
books and ebooks are sold.*

Get 2 Free Books,
Plus 2 Free Gifts—
just for trying the Reader Service!

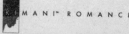

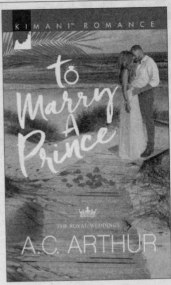